ACCESS

AN ALEX DRAKE NOVEL

LEXXI JAMES

To my partner in crime, Mr. E.
Thank you for reading this romance novel more times than anyone else,
and for always being my Clark Kent.

CHAPTER 1

MADISON

Madison Taylor was always on time, yet today of all days, she was edging dangerously close to being late for an interview she'd wheedled her way into getting. The job opening hadn't even been announced. Instead, she'd come upon it in the happenstance, chain-of-events way so many great opportunities tend to occur.

And it was all thanks to a very pissed-off but well-dressed lady ranting nonstop on her Bluetooth in the bathroom last week.

The woman, oblivious to the presence of anyone else during her conversation, had chattered on and on. Unbothered by the occasional hand-washer or intermittent flushing, she kept talking, and her conversation had captured Madison's undivided attention. From inside her own stall, of course.

"Fuck that bastard. So I took a few bucks from his wallet? Like he'd miss it between buying companies and islands and shit. I type a hundred forty words per minute and do the work of three people while looking smoking hot in my fifteen-hundred-dollar blazer . . . and they fire me? Drake Global Industries can kiss my perfectly Brazilian-waxed ass."

Her blazer costs fifteen hundred bucks? That's almost a month's rent!

Honestly, Madison had long since stopped peeing, but she couldn't tear herself from the seat. From the slit between the door and the wall, she watched the woman in her unmistakable red-bottomed Louboutins pace in and out of view.

Ms. Dressed-to-Impress barely breathed between expletives as she continued her tirade.

Avoiding confrontation had become Madison's happy place. Normally, any amount of shouting was the surest way to an armful of hives. And being raised by a gunnery sergeant dad hadn't exactly helped matters.

Her nonconfrontational nature was part of the reason her butt stayed planted in place, but not the only one. Deep down, she was way too chicken to ask this woman what she was dying to know, preferring instead to park it in a restaurant bathroom stall, letting her vagina air-dry. Maybe if she lingered a little longer, the universe would satisfy her curiosity.

Who should I contact about the new job vacancy at Drake Global Industries?

In a moment of calm, the woman listened intently, softly twirling the end of a cigarette clockwise, then counter-clockwise between her lips, over and over again.

The no smoking sign was enough of a deterrent to keep her from lighting up, and the activity seemed to satisfy some deep-seated need enough to prevent her from puffing to her heart's content outside, thankfully keeping the conversation within earshot.

"Well, Gina Sawyer can kiss my ass too, because she said under the circumstances, she couldn't give me a reference. What a crock of steaming-hot bullshit!"

Bingo!

That little tidbit was Madison's ticket straight to the big leagues. Or at least a shot at them.

A week later, she'd scored an interview with the very same Gina Sawyer mentioned. Thrilled to learn Ms. Sawyer was the director of human capital at DGI, Madison was doubly ecstatic that the job hadn't actually been advertised.

Her request for an interview was, well, incredibly easy. The guy on the other end of the call, Andi with an *i*, explained that Ms. Sawyer wouldn't be back for a week, but he'd go ahead and pencil Madison in.

"Ms. Sawyer's always saying I need to be more proactive, so I'm taking the bull by the fucking horns. She's out this week, but how will Monday at eight a.m. work?"

"Yes, that'll be great!"

"Monday it is." Clicks followed as Andi tapped furiously on his keyboard before he added a few words of advice. "And don't be late. Ms. Sawyer hates tardiness. She also hates puppies, smiles, and happiness in general. You picking up what I'm putting down? Just email your résumé to our HR account today, and you should be good to go. Good luck."

The butterflies in her stomach fluttered madly as Madison got the picture loud and clear. Sucking in a breath, she reminded herself of his words.

Don't smile. Don't bring up puppies. Be ready for a ball-busting interview. And don't be late.

Early Monday morning and definitely not late, Madison hit the ground running. Literally. She'd been raised in Small Town, USA, where city blocks were just a hop, skip, and a jump long. So she'd never get quite used to the Big Apple, or the concept of New York City blocks. The streets alive with bustling cars and hurried people were formidable, stretching endlessly into the distance.

Confused, she emerged from the subway flustered, realizing she'd gotten off too soon, with three insufferable blocks uptown to go. Shoving her doubts to the very back of her mind, Madison sucked in a can-do breath, determined to push onward and upward.

Three blocks. That's not too bad.

Yeah, if she weren't wearing stilettos.

It wasn't like she had a ton of options. Scrounging around her sparse closet and modest wardrobe for something suitable for an interview, she quickly realized corporate-ready shoes were her shortcoming. After passing over a few casual and workout shoes in her closet, she'd decided the ones on her feet were her nicest, most business-appropriate pair. Even if she showed up a little out of breath, she'd look sharp, professional, and like she belonged in the welcome embrace of corporate America.

Sunny and bright, the morning was electric. Energy pulsed through Madison's veins, pushing her pace to a confident stride. A quick check of her phone confirmed her suspicion. At this rate, she wouldn't just be on time, she'd be early.

For some, a thought like that might have downshifted them to settle into an easygoing stroll. But not Madison, and definitely not today. Each breath filled her with optimism and excitement, and the anticipation of a whole new life.

In no time, the towering Manhattan obelisk that housed Drake Global Industries was straight ahead.

"DGI." She sighed, eyeing the gorgeous building of steel, stone, and glass that stretched clear up to the sky.

Charged with pure adrenaline, she rushed around the corner, ready to push through the entrance and hit the interview head-on. Instead, she smacked into something midstep. Like crashing into a wall, she was stopped cold.

Stunned, she bounced back, realizing she hadn't run into a wall—merely a rock-solid man.

"Watch where you're going," the deep voice grumbled before its owner vanished into the building.

Nearly knocked down, she heard herself meekly shout after him, "Sorry."

On second thought, that jerk should have watched where he was going. Butthead.

There Madison stood, again wallowing in her inability to push back when pushed. Or shoved.

Okay, technically, I ran into him, but still.

It was too late to make a scene anyway. And the tragedy of going another day without standing up for herself was quickly overshadowed by the stain of injustice.

And coffee. The tall, dark-suited man with his brick-wall body had left her a parting souvenir before disappearing behind the double glass doors.

Wincing at the injustice of it all, Madison slammed her eyes shut with a huff. A long, dark stain now streaked down the front of her pristinely pressed white silk blouse beneath the black jacket. Her serious attempt at a power suit was two shakes from being shitcanned.

Lightly brushing off a few drops, she assessed the damage. He hadn't spilled much coffee on her, but what there was had hit all the wrong places, striping every ruffle on its way down. And that wasn't the best part. No, the definite *pièce de résistance* was the slightly familiar and overwhelming scent of bourbon.

Panicked, Madison glanced at her watch. With thirty seconds to spare, she had roughly five minutes to figure something out. In her haste, she nearly slammed into another passerby as she rushed into the building.

Keep it together, girl.

Quickly, she found sanctuary in the nearest restroom. Surrounded by the opulence of the marble floors and gold-trimmed faucets, she grumbled mentally that the only way she'd be more out of place would be if she were wearing athleisure wear and flip-flops.

Appalled, she stared at her reflection.

Her hair, which had been so beautifully swept up less than ten minutes ago, was now in shambles. Although part of its condition might be attributable to her brisk three-block jog, the rest was the definite result of the wrestling-federation-caliber body slam.

Half the clips she'd carefully placed now dangled pathetically from loose wisps of hair. The remainder were gone, leaving no hope of recreating the polished and professional updo Madame YouTube had helped her through.

Her black suit itself seemed fine. Twisting to the left and right, Madison nodded, pleased with the condition of the bargain find. But the blouse wasn't so lucky.

With a skunk stripe down the front and all the aromatics of an Irish pub, the only plausible explanation would be that her day drinking had begun well before the crack of dawn.

In a frantic whirl of sheer determination, she stripped her blazer away, ridding herself of the blouse just as someone walked in. Breezing by Madison, the sophisticated woman made her way to a far end stall, shaking her head in disapproval. Another *sorry* escaped Madison's lips before she could help herself.

Determined to keep the tiniest tear restrained, she closed her eyes and took a deep, calming breath.

Do not panic.

Momentarily centered, she looked around. Her last streak of luck from a semipublic bathroom led to today's interview. Staring her reflection down with the right blend of tenacity and naivety, she forced herself onward.

Let's do this.

Biting her pouting lower lip, she shoved her only silk blouse deep in her purse, crossing her fingers in the hope she could rescue it with a soak in the kitchen sink later. Sighing, she hoped her Michael Kors bag wouldn't permanently reek of *eau de booze*. Breathing in a cautious whiff, she desperately wished the zipper still worked.

Making a hasty check of her lacy nude camisole, she found it was thankfully unscathed. The upside of all those semi-outdated but adorable ruffles on the blouse? They managed to soak up every last drop of java, sparing her undergarment. Without over-thinking it, she slipped the black blazer back on, securing it with the single silver button.

Turning this way and that, she sized up her new look. Her impressive cleavage totally nailed it. For naughty librarian, she had the job. But for a Fortune 50 company, it wasn't exactly the ideal interview ensemble.

Pulling back her shoulders, she stood proud and tall. Slowly, her composure crumbled. Then more intentionally, leaving her to hunch forward completely.

I give up.

As usual, Madison's boobs were front and center, always drawing more attention than she preferred. Convincingly optimistic, she nodded.

It's totally fine. This will work.

But as her insecure fingers kept fidgeting with the blazer, trying without success to hide her cleavage, a flush reminded her that her time was up.

Ms. Sawyer hates tardiness replayed over and over in Madison's head, looping steadily to the beat of her thumping heart.

Quickly, she yanked the remaining hair clips from her hair, tousling her wavy locks and letting them gently cascade in a *just got out of bed* look that went beautifully with her peekaboo breasts.

Determined not to care, Madison sucked in a breath and raced out the door, rushing to the front desk with barely a minute to spare.

CHAPTER 2

MADISON

A bit out of breath, Madison arrived at the security desk. "Hi, I'm here for an interview with Ms. Sawyer."

The guard nodded with barely a glance at her and picked up the phone. His badge displayed his name and title—fife, chief of security. The man was intimidating from every angle, but his smile softened him enough just enough to be approachable.

He wrapped up the quick call, clearing Madison for access. As he stood to give her directions, he finally took her in and his mouth dropped open, practically hitting his desk with a clang.

Flustered, Madison breathed through her embarrassment as his eyes steadily focused on her breasts. Suddenly aware of each of her heaving breaths in and out from her brisk jaunt over, she refrained from crossing her arms over her chest. A move like that would just draw even more attention.

Clearing her throat, she straightened her blazer, trying to calm both her breathing and her nerves. Ignoring Fife's annoying grin that thankfully was drool-free, she took the keycard he handed her.

"What's this?" she asked, waving the rigid plastic back and forth to break his hypnotic glare at her boobs.

"Oh." He shook off his watchful fascination. "Um, when you get in the elevator, hold it in front of the magnetic pad on the wall. It's your access to the executive suites. Press *E* after the pad turns blue."

With a soft *thanks*, she hurried over to the glass-walled elevator and got in. There, a bright silver pad glowed blue as soon she waved the keycard in front of it. Only one of the elevator buttons lit up.

A second after Madison pressed *E*, the elevator whisked upward with a soft whirring sound. From the growing height, the lobby looked beautiful as beams of morning sunlight bounced off the marble floors and metal-accented furnishings. She'd been much too distracted to take notice when she entered, but the glass skyscraper and its dancing sunbeams left her breathless.

As the ground level retreated and the people bustling along it shrank into tiny little specks, she started wondering what exact floor she was going to.

With a quick glance at the panel, she realized there were fifty-one marked buttons that hadn't lit up. The bright blue *E* made fifty-two.

As the humming faded and the elevator slowed, Madison sucked in a deep breath, swallowing hard as it stopped. A melodic ping hit the air, and the doors slid open to reveal a large foyer. Soft music played faintly in the background, and a clean but subtle fragrance reminded her of a hotel where she'd briefly worked.

The receptionist sat at a large desk straight ahead. Far ahead. Nearly a New York City block ahead.

Slumping her shoulders, Madison didn't have to check her watch. By this point, she was definitely late.

With a few rushed steps forward, she winced as the clickety-clack of her heels on the polished marble echoed. In this expanse of an outrageously grand entryway, every tap was painfully obnoxious.

Madison tried masking the noise with a rapid succession of tiptoed steps, which only worsened the effect and ended with her tripping over her own feet as she practically swan-dived into the desk.

With catlike reflexes and a big mental thank-you to whoever was watching over her, she caught herself. Smiling, she stood up straight and held out her hand to shake that of the preoccupied woman behind the desk.

The receptionist kept her hands to herself and greeted her with barely a look. "Good morning, Ms. Taylor. Ms. Sawyer is ready for you." With the slightest nod backward, she directed Madison toward the glass-enclosed office behind her.

Timidly, Madison looked up, just then noticing the eyes of the no-nonsense woman locking on hers. Even from across the room, through walls of thick glass and a receptionist desk between them, the woman's cold glare was abso-freaking-lutely intimidating.

Madison imagined being part of a *National Geographic* documentary, where the cheetah, ready to tear the poor defenseless gazelle to smithereens, pauses. Patiently, the cheetah waits, bearing witness as the gazelle fumbles wildly, desperately trying to re-posture itself in some lame attempt to be slaughter-worthy.

Even through the transparent wall, the woman's popped brows showed every bit how very much undecided she remained on the matter.

Rebalanced, Madison moved toward the office and let out the smallest gasp as she wobbled. Clear as day, she felt it. One of her heels was loose, torn a little from the sole.

Dammit, I love these heels.

As carefully and as quickly as possible, she walked over, limping a little to inconspicuously keep her shoe on.

With soft brunette curls and a hard-as-nails grimace, Ms. Sawyer remained on a phone call. She looked up briefly but didn't otherwise acknowledge Madison. "All I know is if you can't have drivers on time for your biggest client, I have ten other companies ready for the work."

Oh, perfect. Ms. Sawyer's already upset. Nervous, Madison hid her jitters behind a shy smile.

With the phone call ended, Ms. Sawyer pursed her lips, seeming to consider her alternatives before finally gesturing an impatient wave toward the chair, impolitely indicating Madison might sit.

Holding in a breath, Madison sat as properly and straightly as possible. The scene began to take on some twisted version of Alice in Wonderland. *Take this breath, and my breasts get bigger. Take the next, and my blazer shrinks smaller, smaller, smaller.*

Between struggling through every stifled breath and her feet absolutely killing her, she just wanted this day to be over already.

gina sawyer was engraved on an intricate crystal nameplate, centrally displayed on the front of her cherrywood desk. The oversized desk could have easily doubled as a dining table, but the top remained unsettlingly bare.

Only a Louis Vuitton planner and a space-age screen sat front and center. She fiddled with a thin golden pen as she made faces at her computer screen.

Pronounced in her eye roll, Ms. Sawyer commenced the interview in a bored singsong voice, repeating a line she'd obviously said a time too many. "So, why do you want to work at Drake Global Industries?"

Quick as a whip and fully prepared, Madison gushed about all things DGI, rattling off market-share statistics and historic accolades like a pro. Her advanced degree in googling set her on a sure path to success. Hopefully, Ms. Sawyer would be wowed and impressed, and practically fall all over herself with "When can you start?"

But even if Ms. Sawyer wasn't, Madison couldn't help but be a little impressed with herself. Raving about how DGI had paved the path for technological innovations in global telecommunications, she desperately wanted to be a part of it. A part of something interesting and important, and so much bigger than this small-town girl in the heart of New York.

Thanks to the publicity churn of an overexposed company, Madison was on her game. Her recitation was half shareholder's presentation, half sermon, as she ambled down the path of how DGI was postured for enterprising leaps in the next era. Despite her enthusiasm, her well-rehearsed speech was abruptly cut off.

"Look, cut the crap. What do you really want?"

Ms. Sawyer's tone was cutting and confrontational, causing Madison to freeze. Blubbering incoherently, she stammered as her voice finally betrayed her, completely giving out.

Her sudden case of speechlessness somehow provoked her unexpected nemesis, who gave her an irate glare. Turning back to her monitor with a few annoyed blinks, Ms. Sawyer tapped at the keyboard tucked beneath the surface of her desk.

"Obviously, I didn't clear you for this interview, and my *former* assistant seems to have gotten the last laugh after all."

Squinting, she scrutinized the screen.

"Basic background investigation. Madison Taylor. Temping for the last year here and there. Barely any college. And, oh yes, all the while moonlighting as a waitress in the evenings, which I'm assuming is to make whatever ends you have meet."

Madison could feel the flush rise up her face. Hearing her less than impressive credentials read aloud was bad enough, but it wasn't like she'd tried hiding anything. So, why did she suddenly feel exposed and embarrassed? And ashamed?

Of course, her break into the big leagues was a bit too good to be true. Hearing her lackluster credentials aloud, she realized her hopes were obviously idiotic.

Why would anyone give me a chance?

Ms. Sawyer's eyes locked on Madison's helpless gaze. Swallowing her uneasiness, Madison slowed her breathing to suppress the tears welling up. Any second now, the flood was coming.

Don't cry. Don't cry.

Clasping her hands, Ms. Sawyer leaned in. "Look, it's not the lack of experience, though, that doesn't help. As impressive as the long list of minimum-wage jobs are, that's not what's really keeping us from making a love connection today. Oh, and it's not even, well, all this."

She gestured with a frown at Madison's blazer and camisole, taking in a deep whiff.

"It's the glorious combination of all of it wrapped up in an obvious overindulgence of night-to-day boozing it up. As much as I hate good-byes, I'm afraid this is the end of the road."

Dismissing Madison without a word, Ms. Sawyer returned to her computer, typing away and decidedly going on to more important matters.

Madison couldn't help but wipe a few determined tears from her eyes as she stood. "Sorry to have wasted your time," she said, her voice wavering. Pressing her weight on that wobbly heel, she needed a moment.

Sorry? Again? Really? What the hell do I have to be sorry for?

Fueled by a fury that wouldn't be ignored, she huffed out a long, pissed-off breath.

She'd already said sorry to the rock-solid waste of a suit whose splash of coffee helped her blow this interview. Then to Little Miss Judgey in the bathroom. Now her chronic apologizing was to the high-and-mighty Gina Sawyer. And for what? A high work ethic and getting body-slammed by a Neanderthal?

Despite Madison's puffed-up posture, ready to give this woman a piece of her mind, Old Stonewall Sawyer hadn't moved. Instead, she seemed perfectly content to continue ignoring Madison. It was just the tipping point to make her blood boil over.

Loudly, she cleared her throat, then bit the inside of her cheek to keep the stubborn little tears from flooding out.

"Hey!" she said loudly, but there was no response. "You know what?"

When Ms. Sawyer continued to ignore her, Madison decided she had to keep going. In a miserable attempt to steady her voice, she squeaked out, "I'm not sorry. You people think you can look down on all us hard workers who make your day better, no matter how crappy our day is going."

Getting a head of steam, Madison kept going, her voice firming more by the second. "And by the way, you missed a few jobs on that background investigation. I worked at Starbucks to pay for those college classes, making hot venti lattes for cold-blooded people like you. And I cleaned bathrooms and scrubbed toilets at a few restaurants you've probably frequented, so say what you want because I'm used to your shit."

Whipping the silk blouse from her purse, she waved it high and proud like the goddamned American flag, and Ms. Sawyer finally deigned to look up.

"Oh, and the reason I look and smell like *this*," Madison said, wildly gesturing at her own spilled-out breasts, "is because another jack-hole who works in this building crashed into me on my way in, dousing my beautiful clearance-sale white Chanel blouse with a full-on hit of his Kentucky coffee. So, I'm not sorry for any of it. I'm just sorry I wasted my time coming up fifty-two floors only to break my heel, when I should've shoved it up your executive butt."

Proudly thrusting out her lingerie-clad chest, she whirled around, standing tall with her dignity as she made her grand exit. Within a few steps, Madison heard Ms. Sawyer's phone buzz, and her bravado faded.

Only then did it occur to her that while she was giving her version of the preamble to the Constitution, high-and-mighty

Ms. Sawyer was probably instant-messaging security. Nervously, Madison quickened her unsteady pace to the elevator.

"Ms. Taylor!" Ms. Sawyer called out.

Oh God, she's going to tell me there are cops waiting for me in the lobby. Maybe threaten me with jail on some trumped-up charge to satisfy her sadistic pleasure. And without a doubt, she'll top it off with the elite cherry of that smug-ass smirk.

Ignoring her name being called, Madison made a beeline to the elevator, desperately stabbing at the call button over and over until the door opened. Inside, she hit the *G*, but the elevator refused to move.

Ms. Sawyer raced out of her office. "Hey! Wait a minute!"

Why won't the door close? Oh, the access card.

Madison feverishly waved it and *G* lit up. With a single tap of the now blue button, the car dropped, swiftly arriving at the lobby. Relief poured out of Madison with an audible breath as the doors opened.

Composed, she pulled herself together, stepping out slowly and carefully in her haphazard attempt at a sophisticated gait in a wobbly shoe.

Halfway to the exit, she heard her name again.

"Ms. Taylor!" Miraculously, Ms. Sawyer was now in the lobby, barely an arm's length from Fife.

How the hell did she get here so fast?

Laser-focused on the exit, Madison picked up the pace. As coolly as her weak stiletto heel would let her, she set her sights on the door.

Steps from freedom, that loose little heel bit it, betraying her and landing her squarely on her greatest asset, right in the middle of the lobby floor.

Ms. Sawyer and Fife raced over, looking down at her. *Of course.* Her epic fail of an escape had to be the icing on their cake.

Defeated, Madison softly said, "Look, I'm leaving. You don't need security."

All six feet four inches of Fife bent over, swooped her up like a rag doll, and gently placed her dead center in front of Ms. Sawyer. Face-to-face, Madison gave her a blank stare.

Ms. Sawyer grabbed her hand, shaking it vigorously. "Welcome to DGI, Ms. Taylor."

Confused about what was happening, Madison could feel her brow furl to a tight knot.

Sporting what seemed like a genuine smile, Ms. Sawyer pulled her closer. "You have the job. And call me Gina."

Fife affirmed her new corporate status with a nod and a wink.

CHAPTER 3

ALEX

Thirty minutes earlier

"Where the fuck is my car?"

Alex Drake, the self-made billionaire and world-renowned telecommunications genius, hated being late. Almost as much as he hated being outsmarted or poor, but not nearly as much. Lateness was his downfall. A tragic vulnerability.

At least being late was a supremely rare occurrence, thanks to a zero-tolerance policy and a treasure trove of expensive watches.

The on-again, off-again reminder of his tortured past was making an encore appearance today. His unforgiving heartbeat pounded through his body, making his hands tremble and deafening his ears. It was an inescapable reminder.

It was the one vulnerability that never let up. Never gave him a break.

Lately, it had taunted him more and more, always lurking just below the surface, ready to emerge when he least suspected it. Still, he should know by now it would happen at the most inconvenient times and places.

Checking his vintage Omega Speedmaster, Alex breathed out a quiet *fuck*. Crumpling in the middle of the crowded sidewalk outside his own goddamn building would be fucking inconvenient, for sure. He could practically see the headline.

CEO COLLAPSES UNDER THE WEIGHT OF BEING A COLOSSAL
DICKHEAD

Technically, he wasn't late. He was early. But with his irritation and edginess ratcheting up beyond control, the fists hidden deep in his pockets balled tighter.

The signs were all too familiar. A panic attack was coming, and faster than usual. *Too fast.*

With a desperate sip from his disposable cup, he found his recent tactic to self-medicate was failing. A few shots of bourbon in his fresh Sumatra just wasn't cutting it this morning, and every staggered breath meant he was running out of time.

He couldn't wait for a car.

Furious beyond reason—because the last thing this circumstance called for was being rational—he hit the third favorite on his phone.

"If I have a driver on call 24/7, then why the hell am I standing on the street corner like an asshole? New driver! Now!"

A tremor ran through his body, forcing him to make a hasty return to his building. His last-second about-face resulted in his solid build flicking off whoever just bounced into him.

Goddammit. "Watch where you're going."

Barely hearing the faint *sorry* above the roar in his ears and what was becoming an intolerable blaring of the busy street, he hightailed it inside. Blinded by every glimmer of light, he had to get away. *Now.*

Sucking in a deep breath, he bolted back into the building. *My building.* Manhattan's testament to his empire. And today, his sanctuary.

With few in his inner circle, no one knew the real Alex Drake. The ones who called him AJ were few and far between.

The man he'd been when DGI was just a pipe dream called Drake Cable & Comm seemed like a lifetime ago. The little garage start-up-that-could took jobs in high-risk areas of the globe, amassing market share and quick cash.

It was a path built from unprecedented financial gains, but at what cost? Risks were easy when you didn't care if you lived or died. The more dangerous the venture, the better. His track record was flawless, save for the single greatest, most devastating personal loss of his life.

Others might have forgiven him. *That's their call. Not mine.*

Hyperfocused to the max, Alex had built his life around profits and deals, filling every void with cash—and the voids were deep and vast. He'd long ago buried any hope for healing or redemption. For happiness. Or love.

To his credit, climbing to the top without outright annihilating others was preferred, but some things were unavoidable. Such is life. And if Alex Drake was anything, that son of a bitch was a fast learner.

A decade ago, life converged at the intersection of crush or be crushed.

Even if the crushing was just the weight of the world around him, hardening his armor was nothing more than a natural measure of self-defense. He could preserve the bits and pieces of the old Alex, pushing onward while saving whatever slivers could be spared in the aftermath.

The problem was, he'd become the only inmate of his custom-tailored luxury prison. No matter how gilded, all prisons are ultimately lonely.

"Good morning, Mr. Drake," rang across the lobby from the usual choir.

Detached and determined to keep his stride brisk, he held it together just long enough to refrain from a full-blown run.

His feet picked up the pace as he closed in on his private elevator tucked behind the security desk. Intentionally, it was designed to blend invisibly behind the wall.

As he swiped the access panel, his hand squeezed the embossed platinum-plated access card until his knuckles turned white. Without looking, he knew his embossed initials on the corner would be imprinted on his palm. This wasn't his first rodeo through the past.

At the fifty-second floor, he stepped through the door to his lavish penthouse office overlooking Central Park. The sweeping views of lush trees and tranquil water were always enough to capture and calm him. At least, for the moment.

He could always lose himself in the view. The magnificence of it soothed his heartbeat, luring him from the heavy toll and endless anxiety that empire-building and burying a past tended to bring.

After a few meditative breaths, he was relieved when his mind cleared. Stronger, he could come to grips with dealing with the day. A sudden jolt in his pulse kicked his instincts into high gear.

It's not over. Proceed with caution.

What if I was out when it happened? Not somewhere . . . safe?

Quickly, he scrolled through his phone, frowning as he clicked the contact of a higher-ranking favorite.

"Paco. You need to take a meeting for me. Check my calendar. Twenty minutes. The usual place."

He didn't bother thanking his stand-in. The man knew the deal and understood. *He always understands.*

Suddenly free for an hour or so, Alex eased into the seat at his oversized desk, running a hand across the smooth wood surface. He sucked in a deep breath with an entirely new wave of thoughts awakening.

Again, his pulse quickened. Different from the blood-pressure spike on the street, this wasn't unwelcome. His lips curled up as he reminisced about all the tantalizing women he'd had bent over the custom-carved cherrywood desk.

Seeking the company of a beautiful woman was unnecessary. The endless string of luscious distractions always sought him out, appearing from out of nowhere, and in spades. He could take them or leave them, allowing himself the indulgence when the mood struck him. And showing them the door when the mood was over.

Exchanging numbers never happened. He'd make do with the not-so-cheap thrills an abundance of nameless, faceless ladies could provide. And the desk in front of him? It was the only part of his life he'd let them close to. His demand for privacy was unyielding, and his home was strictly off-limits. No one got close to him there, because no one got close to him. Period.

Call it unprofessional, but the lap of his empire's luxury seemed to satiate everyone's needs. And satisfaction was guaranteed, at least for the much younger ladies.

Come. Don't come. He didn't care. In the end, they walked away with a sweet kiss, his boyish grin, and a nice little something-something from Cartier as a quick consolation prize and very final farewell.

After checking his watch, he sent a direct message.

ALEX: Gina, I need that new driver ready for lunch at Le Bernardin.

GINA: On it. And he'll be early.

ALEX: I'm sure he will. You have a definite je ne sais quoi with our service contractors. Must be your remarkable charm.
Speaking of which, how's your new assistant?

GINA: Oh, you need to see for yourself.

Curious, Alex flipped on his monitor. Years ago, some lunatic demanded his contract be paid in full, and when Gina refused, he pulled a knife on her. Earning herself the nickname Tough as Nails, she talked him off the ledge. But the whole incident pissed everyone off, no one more than Tough as Nails herself.

At the end of the day, DGI didn't have enough to prosecute or sue. Sadly, it was her word against his. A week later and at Gina's rather loud insistence, cameras were installed in key locations throughout the skyscraper, with several in and around her office.

Spying on employees wasn't exactly Alex Drake's speed. When necessary, he had people for that. But every now and again, Gina would rope him into something sure to lift his spirits.

Alex moved closer to the monitor and with a two-fingered swipe, expanded the view.

ALEX: Is she holding what I think she's holding?

GINA: Yup.

Fascinated, Alex watched the young assistant with her hands below the desk, hastily scrambling and unscrambling a Rubik's cube, over and over again, and checking her watch after each go.

ALEX: She's fast. Competition level. So, are you thinking what I'm thinking?

GINA: Well, I'm thinking she's not the sharpest pin in the cushion. I mean, she's trying to hide what she's doing, holding her hands under the desk. And yet she's oblivious to the fact that the wall behind her is made entirely of glass. Obviously, I can see everything.

After a second, the dancing bubbles began again.

GINA: I'm predicting I'm about to lose an assistant, and not because I get the benefit of firing her cubing ass. Nope, you're going to poach yet another one of my assistants for other areas of the firm.

ALEX: It's like you're in my head. Any military background?

Smiling, Alex watched Gina's shoulders slump, letting her head fall back in exaggerated defeat. She dragged her keyboard to her lap, and her fingers flew across the keys.

GINA: Yes. Secret clearance. Music to your ears. Geeks unite. So, where's this one going?

Watching the assistant's next spin whirl faster than the last, Alex rubbed his chin with his thumb.

ALEX: Not sure yet. Get with the assessment team and see if there's any aptitude for coding or crypto.

GINA: Of course. Since I've had her for a week, why not?

He practically heard every note of her irate tone.

ALEX: Hey, I'm saving you from serious jail time. Another few days of watching this, and you'd strangle the kid with your bare hands. And it's not just geeks. Justin Bieber can spin a cube in under two minutes.

GINA: Fine. If you're done sharing how you and the Biebs have so much in common, I need to call the car service before my next appointment. My boss will do his own murdering if they're late.

Amused, he couldn't help a slight chuckle that Gina was this peeved. Leaving it at that was completely out of the question. He teed up an easy shot that would ease her mood.

ALEX: Aw, c'mon. Tell me how you really feel?

With no more prompting, Gina moved her hand inconspicuously behind her head, as if to fix her hair. Discreetly, she used the opportunity to show Alex how he was "number one."

Somehow, the international sign for *go fuck yourself* always made a grin spread across his face. Not too long ago, Gina let it slip that she never imagined her request for monitors would lead to giving her boss the finger more often than not. She confessed it was a total perk.

Getting flipped off usually meant the webcast was over, but the elevator opening caught his eye. Stunned, Alex couldn't take his eyes off the screen.

Even across the distance and through the glass walls, Gina's cameras picked up the shapely legs and voluptuous body of a whole new mesmerizing, delicious distraction.

What do we have here?

Like Fife before him, Alex fixated on the hypnotic lull of her beautiful porcelain breasts, firm yet softly jiggling with her every suggestive step.

Something about her gait seemed nervous. Unsure? Unusual with the overly confident lot of candidates that came and went.

Closing in on the reception desk, the shy little temptress tripped, eliciting a subtle laugh from a nearly giddy Alex.

Oh, there goes her heel.

His hand hovered over the monitor's power button, not quite ready to shut it off. He cursed the fuzzy video feed, making him wish he'd invested in a slightly higher resolution system.

The scene unraveled, bit by tantalizing bit. By Gina's thoroughly unamused demeanor, she was about to do what she did best.

Gina wasn't exactly hired for her people-pleasing skills. She was essentially a behemoth of a gatekeeper, defending his corporate fortress like a 300-pound bouncer. Whoever the scantily clad Ms. Blazer was, Alex knew one thing for certain. She was on her way to being bounced out.

But, God, what a beautiful bounce it would be.

Front and center for a showdown, he ignored the erratic spikes in his heart rate. Consequences be damned, his eyes were staying glued to the screen.

Fuck, look at her. How can I not?

Every alluring sway of her body tantalized him, and the relentless throbbing in his pants pressed with need. This pretty young thing was well on her way to getting her perfectly round ass handed to her on a platter, and he ached to be the tray.

But something else held his unblinking gaze. Something about this girl was different. Interesting. Undeniably magnetic. With a strange familiarity that made his mind race.

Her sweet pouty smile sent his head into overdrive. He could imagine it in about a billion different scenarios. And the longer he stared, the dirtier each naughty little thought became.

Transfixed, he propped an elbow on the desk, resting his chin on his fist. Sooner than expected, she stood, obviously unhappy. Unsatisfied, he frowned at the completely anticipated conclusion.

He huffed under his breath, disappointed at the premature end to their brief and very one-sided time together.

I give it twenty-four hours. If I can't get her out of my head, Gina always has her contact information.

After taking a single step to the door, the woman whipped her body around. The beautiful dancer-like turn stole his breath and caused him to raise a brow.

A second later, her demeanor transformed from a polite little interviewee into one hell of a half-naked fireball, exaggerating every movement and capturing his wide-eyed amusement.

Fuck me. Naughty librarian. Nailed it.

He turned the volume louder. Catching the tail end of his little spitfire going on and on about how Gina was an asshole made his smile widen.

Yup! Gina hasn't lost her touch.

His thumping pulse reminded him again how his unpredictable state could spiral out of control at any moment. With a deep understanding that there were worse ways to go, he sucked in a calming breath but stayed glued to the screen.

Lifting the warm cup to his lips, he filled his mouth with a healthy swig, savoring the flavor. Transfixed by her feisty moves and delicious jiggles, Alex ignored the subtle pounding in his ears.

"Oh," she said loud and clear, punctuating her words around a semi-erotic dance of wild gestures. "The reason I look and smell like *this . . .*"

God, don't stop moving like that!

". . . is because another jack-hole who works in this building crashed into me on my way in, dousing my beautiful clearance-sale white Chanel blouse with a full-on hit of his Kentucky coffee."

Shit. Instantly, Alex's grin vanished. Forcing down the mouthful of the Woodford-spiked Indonesian Sumatra, he swallowed his guilt with an audible gulp.

I'm the jack-hole.

A second later, he panicked as she scurried away. His fingers couldn't hit Gina's number fast enough.

"Gina, hire her. Now!"

"Yes, Mr. D." Gina's shout was loud, making its way to his ear just as she killed the call. "Ms. Taylor!"

Holy fuck. What did she say?

Snatching the screen, he spat out a few more expletives, aggravated that *Ms. Taylor* was hightailing it farther and farther away. Before Gina could reach her, the main elevator was carrying her swiftly to the ground floor.

Intently, he watched the scene unfold. Gina was doubling back, scurrying toward his office. A step ahead of her, he flung his office door wide.

Before Gina could ask, he nodded a hurried approval. With that, she flew past his office, stealing his private elevator for the hot pursuit.

Relieved and a little rattled, he blew a huge sigh through his lips as he rubbed at the tension in the back of his neck.

Resting against his door until it closed, the name that launched a thousand one-night stands echoed through his mind.

Ms. Taylor.

In a last-ditch attempt to stomp out his growing hopes, he reminded himself that *Taylor* was a common enough name. Hell, with his trail of conquests, he should know.

Maybe it was of no consequence. At all. Just another dead end. It's not like his diligence in working through the on-again-off-again Taylor-of-the-Month club ever panned out.

But he couldn't shake it . . . *that* feeling.

I have to know.

Unconvinced he hadn't toppled over into certifiable insanity, he teed up a text to Paco, then paused. *What the hell is her first name?*

With a quick check of Gina's calendar, he had it. And decidedly, he liked it. A smile settled on his lips as he whispered, "Madison."

ALEX: Need you to check out a woman.

PACO: Women are your area. Not mine.

ALEX: Last name Taylor.

PACO: Taylor? Sure. It's been a hot second since the last dozen

Taylors I've checked out. But at the moment, I'm a little busy covering someone's ass at a meeting.

Smug and confident, Alex didn't respond. He didn't have to. He just needed to take a breath, sit back, and let Paco come to the decision he always came around to.

PACO: First name?

ALEX: Madison.

The bubbles on his phone screen bounced, then stopped, then bounced again. Impatient, Alex huffed, knowing that Paco was in a vicious cycle of typing, erasing, retyping, re-erasing. Finally, his text arrived.

PACO: How about you take the day off?

ALEX: How about you fuck off?

Insistently, his phone buzzed. *Of course.*

Who knows what excuse Paco came up with to tear himself away from the meeting. Likely, his discreet under-the-table texting wouldn't convey the exact message Paco needed transmitted. No doubt, he wanted to talk Alex off the ledge.

What he didn't know was that Alex was in the throes of freefalling into the familiar hold of a full-on manic state.

Heated, he answered the call. "Need to hear me say it? Fuck off!"

"Seriously, I'm worried about you. No bullshit. You've got to let this go."

Alex paused just long enough to avoid lashing out and going completely ape-shit on the man. "I hear what you're saying. Now try hearing me. Mad-i-son Tay-lor. Just . . . find out."

Even he was annoyed at the unexpected whine in his tone. Cutting the conversation short, Alex hung up.

Uncertain he was doing the right thing, he dragged his hands across his mouth and cheeks, settling there in disbelief. Paco's great advice was quickly shoved to the sidelines. His mind was made up.

I'm right this time. I can feel it.

The talk with Paco reignited his edginess. With a watchful eye, he monitored the mild tremble in his hands. Glaring, he willed it to stop, and a second later, it did. The surprise made him content, but not cocky. But the pounding was still there, deep in his head.

Out of habit, he rubbed his brow before lowering his hands to his temples. Applying light circles of pressure to the throbbing, he knew he couldn't spend the rest of the day ping-ponging out of control and between emotional extremes.

With a ton of meetings that would take him well into the evening, he needed to get it together. Paco couldn't take all of them. *Focus.*

Oh, he was focused, all right.

Madison Taylor. His eyes closed as doubt crept in. *Could it be her? What are the odds?*

Even if she's not *the* Taylor, the draw to *this* Taylor was indescribable. Compelling.

Or is it just that she's attractive? Very attractive.

Sexy? With her lush locks lying across those breasts ready to bust loose, Alex took a breath. *Definitely sexy.*

But he'd seen sexy a hundred times over. What was it that made her different? Perhaps the way her raw emotions played out in every passionate move was enough to captivate him.

The vision of her behind his eyes was still so fresh. So ready. He could use it. Calm the erratic energy surging through every part of his body. A willing hostage, his mind surrendered completely to thoughts of her. And once again, his pulse spiked.

If he didn't get a grip before lunch, the meeting that took months to arrange would be sunk.

So, why not? Get a grip, that is.

Too much was on the line, and a quick run was out of the question. Low on options and time, Alex took hold of the perfect pressure valve, ready for a release.

Fuck it. She's perfect. She's mine.

Eager to lose himself in thoughts of her, he rested back in his chair. Instantly, his shoulders relaxed as his emotions drifted from wonder to desire. Visions of her beautiful breasts and full lips filled his mind.

The throbbing readily shifted from his head, rushing down to his other head. His cock bulged hard against his pants, eager for an escape.

"Dim." The bright lights of his office softened and the shades lowered, covering the panoramic views. Covering the bases, he called out, "Lock," and the bolt on his office door engaged, giving him the privacy he needed.

Unzipping his trousers, Alex caressed the heaviness in his hand, easing back into the reclining seat.

His eyes closed, he stroked, succumbing to the tantalizing vision of those pouty, luscious lips. Soft skin. Gorgeous ass that begged for his touch. He imagined how her seductive moans would fill the air as he peeled the blazer from her skin.

Tugging that suggestive camisole down, he'd quell a fiery, hard nipple with his mouth, suckling gently, then harder in the moment. His rod would press slowly through her willing, full lips.

God, that feels good.

Thoughts of her beautiful mouth made him stroke faster. Alex could practically touch her—taste her—the warmth of her mouth was all around his cock. Pumping tight and fast, his own friction built the sensation. Heat spread throughout his body, and his balls tightened.

Rapturous, erotic thoughts flickered through his mind like a film. He had to have her. Take her. Take care of her?

"Yes," pushed through his lips without hesitation. Take care of her as no man had. Or could.

God, what is it about her?

What if everything could change? Be turned right?

It all feels so right.

Intoxicating thoughts of having her—keeping her—closed in on him. He could feel the softness of her delicate hands around him with every stroke. Deep in her mouth, he pumped himself harder.

Make me come, Madison.

His fantasies swallowed him. His balls pulled up as his thighs stiffened, quaking by the orgasm crashing through him, his essence coating her lips and throat. He ignited, slamming his other hand down on the desk. Every tense muscle in his electric body was set free.

The edginess and stress were gone. But so was she.

Breaking from the spell, Alex opened his groggy eyes. Clear as day, he saw the reality of the situation. The only thing he'd coated was a good part of his perfectly tailored Armani pants.

Heaving, he looked around, then barked out, "Time?"

"The time is eleven o'clock," said the seductive automated voice of his virtual assistant.

Barely able to catch his breath, he grabbed a few tissues from the drawer. Swiping at his pants with them, he cursed as he managed to make the streaks noticeably worse.

With an irritated huff, he kicked off his shoes and stood, letting his unsalvageable pants fall to the floor. He slipped off the matching blazer but was content to keep his shirt on.

Taking a staggered step to the wall behind him, he swiped his access card across the panel, habitually slipping it back into the breast pocket of his shirt.

The wall opened, revealing the hidden room. Soft lights

flooded the interior, illuminating a massive closet filled with suits, shirts, shoes, and coats, most still new with tags. Ties from Armani and Gucci hung from an array of hooks, matching the general blues and dark grays of the suits of each meticulously designed and color-coded section.

In the corner was another panel, which also required Alex's access card. With a quick swipe, it opened, revealing three shelves. The top shelf held eight high-end vintage watches. Just the ones he favored.

The second shelf held a cluster of Cartier and Tiffany & Co. boxes. Nothing ends a one-night stand better than a bauble worth more than a car.

Finally, at the very bottom of the secure case was the root of all evil—a staggering pile of cold, hard cash. Crisp new hundred-dollar bills were wrapped in hundred-thousand-dollar stacks of ten-thousand-dollar bundles, neatly assembled in rows.

His jaw was tense with indecision. Abandoning further deliberation, he erred on the side of generous, tearing open a bundle and snatching ten grand free.

Unlike the black suit he'd worn earlier, a deep blue one caught his eye. He nodded approvingly, satisfied with the style and color for the remainder of the day.

It meant his Omega Speedmaster no longer matched. Perusing his options, he half considered a Vacheron Constantin before settling on a Patek Philippe, better matching a sleek belt and new untouched shoes.

Satisfied, he dressed and returned everything to its previously secured state. Then he stepped to an adjacent and rather lavish bathroom where he washed and dried his hands, checking them again for even the subtlest signs of a shake.

Certain the worst of his tremors was over, he straightened the tie that had loosened and made a last once-over of his appearance. Returning to his desk, he leaned over his computer to send one last message.

alex: Gina, have them clean my office before I return.

The time caught his eye. Quickly, he slid the ten-thousand-dollar stack into the pocket of the discarded blazer, ensuring the end of the hundreds were in clear view.

Not giving the cash a second thought, he strolled to his elevator, which had returned, awaiting his arrival. Everything in Alex's life was programmed for his gratification. Well, everything that could be programmed.

He knew that within half an hour, two people would enter his office. Besides the usual wipe down and vacuuming, they'd remove the clothing and shoes from beneath the desk. These two cleaners were the oldest employees of DGI. They'd seen many suits and shoes, though never for this reason.

Gloved, they'd feverishly work. Their jobs were confined to cleaning the executive floor, while the rest of the building was handled by a major contractor.

Whenever they found clothing on the floor, their long-standing and explicit instructions were well understood, but known only to them.

CHAPTER 4

MADISON

A month later

Fast-paced and exciting, Madison's job challenged her in ways she'd never imagined work could. She was originally hired as a management intern, but her intuitive skills in analysis and trending surprised even her. Within two weeks, she'd been reassigned as an executive analyst.

The move was sudden and unexpected. She'd even been presented with a signing bonus. In her mind, signing bonuses were reserved for athletes, recording artists, and people who cleaned up toxic waste.

Thankful for the bonus, she'd caught up on some bills and bought a few new outfits, hedging her bet by holding on to most of her windfall. Doubt always gnawed at the back of her mind. More than anyone, she knew the drill. Life happens, and this dream job might vanish as quickly as it had appeared.

Making the most of every thrilling little bit of DGI life was priority number one. Time flew by as Madison poured herself into work, learning absolutely everything she could about the fascinating company.

Forgoing lunch became a natural consequence of ingesting every ounce of corporate history. Who needs food? Work filled her more completely than anything had in a while.

Passion? Obsession? To-may-to, to-mah-to.

Often the first one in the office, she enjoyed jockeying for position with Fife for who'd be the last one out. Most days, it was Madison for the win.

And to add a ribbon of chocolate to life's three-scoop sundae of a future, the news she'd been on pins and needles waiting on had finally come. Her lease application for a nicer one-bedroom apartment in the heart of the city was approved.

Translation? She could ditch her two party-girl roommates for a centrally located pad overlooking a much quieter street. The one-bedroom apartment was within walking distance of coffee shops, quaint bookstores, and the DGI skyscraper that still filled her with excited little butterflies every time she stepped into it.

Her vision of life in the big city was coming true. It was everything she'd dreamed of when she abandoned a comfy small-town existence for the crazy allure of New York City.

Blame Broadway and every romcom ever featured there.

And coming and going worry-free of traffic gave her a few extra zzz's each day. Not hours, but just enough to let her escape into a steamy romance novel late each night.

With all big cities, there were risks. Despite her hop, skip, and jump to and from work, easy going couldn't always be in the cards.

Three yawns in, Madison stretched in the ergonomic comfort of her office chair and checked her phone. It was late. With a dreamy glance out the window, she noticed the sun was still shining, but barely.

Like most evenings, she crossed the empty lobby, a little *hoorah* leaping into her mind as she spied the empty security desk. *Yes! Four-for-0 this week.* Her title of Last Woman Standing was undisputed.

The silence of the vast lobby was barely broken by the sneakers she'd changed into for the walk home. Not super fashionable, but she really needed to preserve her work heels. Sighing, she still missed her pretty little stilettos. Her personal sacrifice to the great DGI gods.

With a quick flip, she swiped her access card to leave. The building would be locked down after Fife left, and anyone remaining would need to badge out for the door to release.

Rounding the corner of the building, she made a hasty dig in her purse to be sure she had a five-dollar bill, ready to give it to Joe. The homeless man often lingered at the corner at the end of the building. He'd apparently been a staple of the block for years.

Nicknamed G.I. Joe due to the vintage BDU jacket he sported from a war long gone, he was purported to be harmless. But the harmless, homeless veterans were always on her mind, haunting her since the loss of her brother, Jack.

Whenever she could, she'd either give Joe a few bucks or a meal, or both if she could swing it. Today, though, she left the money in her purse when she saw Joe wasn't alone. Tucked into a ball on the sidewalk, Joe could barely defend himself against the three guys huddled around him in some jacked-up rugby scrimmage.

Laughing, two of them shoved him with their feet, warning him about returning. A third guy puffed his cigarette through a scowl only a mother could love. His tossing his cigarette at Joe was the last straw for Madison.

Without thinking, she ran up to them, shouting, "Hey, leave him alone!"

The three men turned toward her. Slowly, their sadistic smiles widened as they met her eyes.

Shit, now what?

The big one with the cigarette and disturbingly thick fore-head jeered. "Well, well, well . . . looks like Supergirl has arrived."

Her heart pounding, she gulped hard at his approach.

Before she could step back, another one grabbed her forearm. "How 'bout you let a real man show you a good time?"

Alarmed, she tugged, desperate to be free of his hold, but his firm grip remained wrapped around her wrist. Undeterred, Madison yanked back with the full force of every bit of strength in her body.

She toppled back as if freed, slapping her arm into yet another man. This one caught it.

"What seems to be the problem?"

The low voice boomed with a take-no-shit tone, sending an untimely jolt straight to the very worst parts of her under the circumstances.

Looking up over her shoulder, Madison lost her breath, taking in the ruggedly handsome stranger standing behind her.

Holy crap. It's Alex Drake.

Panicked to find her arm still stuck to his chest like a fridge magnet, she shyly drew it back but he grasped it. Apparently, releasing her wasn't part of his plans. And the longer he held it, the harder it was for her to breathe.

Calmly but firmly, he nudged her behind him, barricading her from the three men with his own body. Only then did she slip from his hold. Stepping forward, he put more space between her and the cluster of bullies.

Starstruck and in disbelief, Madison watched, frozen. She should be running. Getting help. Something. Anything.

But her little tennis-shoed feet weren't budging an inch without his say. Beyond a shadow of a doubt, this man had control. She had no idea what was coming, but every instinct told her whatever he was about to do, she'd never forget it. He was there for one reason.

To protect me.

CHAPTER 5

ALEX

It had been nearly a month since Alex's last episode, but with pure adrenaline pumping through his veins and the Madison of his dreams behind his back, he stood confident. Perhaps arrogantly so.

The risk was worth it. She was more than worth it. And exercise never provoked his condition, so unleashing a righteous asskicking should calm him right down.

"Hey, we were just showing the lady a good time," the biggest asshole said, staring up at Alex.

With a few inches on the guy, Alex smiled as the son of a bitch gave him one hell of a snarl. Reflexes ready and hackles raised, Alex was primed to give him a pounding.

Whether in the back alley or the boardroom, the Hulk in Alex was always ready to pounce. Too ready, which occasionally posed an occupational hazard. But today, all signs pointed to *fuck yeah*. All that adrenaline reinforced him.

The deadly heat of Alex's glare belied his half-cocked smile. Stepping forward, he didn't blink, not stopping until their noses were barely inches apart.

"Well, party's over," he said, a growl lacing his words. "I

suggest you and your minions head on out." Alex's tone was as fair a warning as they were getting, the coil before the strike.

"Hey, no problem." The bastard backed off just enough to pull back a punch.

The lame move was totally expected. And for Alex, it might as well have been in slow motion.

The guy attempted a pathetically wide jab at Alex's head. Sure, Alex was a black belt in three separate martial arts, but none of that was necessary. Swiftly leaning to the right, he eased out of the way just enough to deflect the blow, using his attacker's momentum to shove the guy hard into the granite wall of the side of his building. Full force. Headfirst.

Stunned, his attacker collapsed to his knees, eliciting a stifled chuckle from Alex. Casually straightening his blazer, he then rubbed the wall, coyly checking it for scratches. When he gave the other two a quick stare-down, they backed away, raising their hands in worried surrender.

Behind them, Alex caught two of New York's finest racing over, plus Fife was now rushing to the scene, his usually pleasant demeanor gone. Alex recognized the no-nonsense glare of the former SEAL's combat days.

The two hooligans bolted from the scene, abandoning their friend. The cops grabbed him, forcing him to his feet.

"Not an issue, gentlemen," Alex said, figuring the ass-wipe had probably learned his lesson. That, and the last thing he needed was a crime report at his own goddamn doorstep. "My friend just fell. He's pretty clumsy, so I'm sure he'll tread lightly the next time he walks by this part of town."

Reluctantly, the cops released the douchebag. Grumbling in defeat, the man staggered away.

Determined to make the most of their brisk run over, the cops turned their attention on G.I. Joe. "Hey, buddy, you can't be here. Get going."

Again, Alex intervened, smoothing his words with a cool layer of diplomacy.

"Gentlemen. This guy's not hurting anyone, and by the tiles he's lying across, I believe he's technically on private property. So, unless the owner has an issue, which *I* don't, then under the laws of the State of New York, he's free to lounge, eat, unaggressively panhandle, and discreetly urinate on the building as long as he doesn't expose himself." Alex unleashed his most charming smile. "Gotta love New York City laws, right?"

Dismayed and shaking their heads, the boys in blue looked at each other, then smirked back at Alex and yielded with nods. "Hey," one of them said, "if you want him here, trust us, he's yours. He's a hell of an accessory for your monumental skyscraper."

Their sarcastic laughs thinly veiled their mild irritation.

Annoying the cops hadn't been Alex's intention. Busting their butts each and every day was the life they lived. The last thing they needed was another pompous prick showing them up. He'd never mock their determination to "protect and serve."

Sincere apology sweetened his tone. "Look, I appreciate it. And you. How about when your shift ends, you can be my guests at the 21 Club?" He handed them each his card. "Tonight, or whenever. Just show them this card, and they'll take care of you."

Alex wasn't sure they'd take him up on it, but they thanked him nonetheless. And he'd take care of them one way or another. He always did.

With a glance at their badges, he filed their names away, adding them to a growing list of people to look after. *Someday.*

He shook their hands, then watched them tip their hats to Madison, Fife, and even Joe, before they each pocketed his card and returned the way they came.

"Fife, take Ms. Taylor inside. I'd like a private chat with this guy."

With a step toward Joe, Alex was surprised to be blocked.

Madison moved between them, locking her bright doe eyes straight on him.

"Mr. Drake, I'm so sorry you had to get involved, but I can help him."

Her concern for Joe was obvious from her wide-eyed pleading and the subtle lines in her brow. She was worried, and Alex couldn't believe what it was doing to him.

So many feelings were swirling around inside him, but one raw emotion surged up through him more than anything else. Something he rarely experienced when dealing with people, and even less with women.

For the first time in ages, he was genuinely intrigued.

Madison's concern apparently didn't escape Joe, who'd been sitting silently until that moment.

"Hey, don't worry, doll. AJ will take good care of me."

Madison and Fife looked at Joe, then Alex, obviously confused by Joe's reference.

Their hesitation gave Alex an excuse to lean close to Madison's ear, keeping his voice just above a whisper. "Apparently, I look like someone he knows."

Damn, she smells good.

Still, Madison wasn't budging an inch, and if she kept it up, the bulge in his pants was ready to show her more than an inch.

Firmly, she stood her ground. Based on her crossed arms and stubborn stance, she had no intention of going anywhere.

"Look, Ms. Taylor, I'm not sure why you're so concerned, but you needn't be. He'll be fine."

Alex had a pretty good idea what she was thinking. Between his MMA moves and his hard-charging, no-bullshit reputation, she was apparently afraid to leave him alone with Joe.

A second later, she started pleading. "Mr. Drake, he's a veteran. Please don't hurt him."

Alex couldn't hold back a smile. "I'm not going to hurt him."

A knot formed in her brow, telling him that the object of his little fixation must have thought he was being patronizing. Admittedly, it might have been the tiniest bit patronizing.

The doubt clear on her face was endearing.

Beauty and *balls. Fuck, she's adorable.*

Unable to shed his smug grin, Alex solemnly raised a palm in the air. "I swear to God I won't hurt him."

Madison backed up, as if half expecting a lightning bolt to strike him down from the sky.

With a small step forward, he was in her space. One glance in her big, beautiful eyes stole his breath, and he gripped her upper arms.

The shiver that ran through her body made him want to take her. *Right here, right now, for all the world to fucking see.* But glancing at Fife, and then Joe, he scratched the idea.

Instinctively, he softened his touch, smoothing his thumbs back and forth. It seemed to set her at ease. Her lips parted, audibly catching a shallow breath. And, God, it took every ounce of willpower to keep himself from plunging a deep kiss past a polite pretense and straight down her throat.

Instead, he handed her off to Fife, shooting the man a stern look. "Get her inside."

Fife's arm swooped around her, replacing Alex's grip. As his chief of security pulled Madison safely into the building, Alex watched her twist around to look back. Something in him deflated as he realized she was looking at Joe.

As if on cue, Joe shouted, "Don't worry. AJ and I are gonna catch up."

Once Fife rounded the corner with Madison in tow, Alex again straightened his suit and adjusted his tie, still watching to ensure Madison hadn't doubled back.

Sterner than usual, Alex said, "Joe?"

"Yeah, AJ?"

In a short, casual stroll, Alex stood before Joe, then tugged at his slacks to squat down. The vantage point allowed an eye-to-eye discussion.

Alex let out a slow huff. "You know you can't piss on my building, right?"

Grinning, Joe reassured him. "Right, AJ."

They both enjoyed an extended chuckle as Alex reached into the breast pocket of his suit. He always kept Marlboros in a silver case, although he never indulged. Ready and waiting, they were there to appease various clients and random women who were so inclined.

But today, he pulled one out and offered it to a grateful Joe, lighting it for him and wrapping his hand around it to ensure the light breeze didn't steal the flame before Joe could savor a puff.

Joe relaxed, giving Alex enough leeway to ask a question.

"So, how do you know Supergirl?"

CHAPTER 6

MADISON

"Fife?" Madison said, still reeling from being escorted back into the building like a child.

"Yes, Ms. Taylor?"

"I *was* actually on my way out."

She eyed his hand on her shoulder, and with an uncertain shrug, he promptly removed it.

"Well, I guessed that since you carded out, but Mr. Drake told me to bring you in," Fife said as he headed toward his desk, and she followed.

"I carded out because I thought you were gone."

"I just had to do some paperwork," he said, pointing his large index finger toward the bathroom.

"So, how did you know to come outside?"

"Oh, I saw it all as soon as I returned." Turning the screen, he showed her his monitor, which displayed the live footage from eight separate angles, including the current feed from the exterior.

Scooting next to Fife, she took a better look. The cameras were trained on Alex and Joe. Studying the screen hard, she saw that Alex seemed to be handing Joe a cigarette, then lighting it for him. Their conversation seemed friendly and casual.

Are they laughing? They look like two old friends.

Feeling an inch tall and even worse for wishing there was audio, Madison bit her lip.

How could I have pegged him so wrong?

She knew his history practically by heart. Alex Drake was the founder and CEO of a global multibillion-dollar empire. Yet, she'd considered his intentions to be no better than those of her assailants.

Deeply immersed in the silent conversation, she watched as things seemed to be wrapping up. Madison couldn't help the feelings coming over her. Most of all, she was intrigued.

Alex concluded their chat by pulling out his wallet, then handed Joe what seemed to be its entire contents. The bills were definitely hundreds. A lot of them.

With that, he turned to return to the lobby, sending Fife into a slight panic. With a gentle shove, he moved Madison to the other side of the desk, hiding the fact they'd been watching Alex's "private" conversation.

With the boss approaching, both acted abnormally nonchalant. As Alex stepped closer, Madison couldn't help notice him averting his eyes.

"Ms. Taylor needs a ride home, Fife." Ignoring her and seeming collected but pissed, he said nothing else. And she hated it.

Trying to make amends for having irked the man who had just rescued her, she forced herself into the conversation.

"Mr. Drake, I can't thank you enough for what you did back there, but a company car isn't necessary."

His deep breath was audible, and the air of annoyance surrounding it was almost more than she could bear.

He looked back, hardening his eyes with a glare. "You might not feel it's necessary, but when I see people on my staff getting manhandled right on my property, let's just say I'm not letting you traipse home alone."

"I meant I can get a Lyft. I don't want you or the company further inconvenienced."

"This isn't a debate, Ms. Taylor."

The pesky little hives growing beneath her sleeve were an instant response to his loudness.

"You want to lose your fucking mind and stand between a homeless guy and three thugs intent on beating the crap out of someone, next time do it off my property. It's a liability to this company . . . and to me. So, unless you've got some badass kung-fu skills you can whip out from beneath that skirt, I strongly suggest you take the car."

Abruptly, he ended the conversation, heading toward the executive garage. Before the door shut behind him, he repeated himself. "Get her the car, Fife."

Watching him walk away, which did she hate more? Him for being a total bastard, or herself for having a hand in making him one?

Fife stepped up, interrupting her internal debate. "You'd actually be doing me a big favor if you let me drive you home. My car's a little sketchy right now, and that means I get a company car for the evening. Okay?"

Nodding, she let out a sigh. "Yes, of course. Thanks."

Once in the car, Fife yammered on and on, giving it his all to reassure her. "Hey, don't let it get to you. Mr. Drake might be a rich blowhard, but he's a blowhard that cares, and that should count for something, right?"

Forcing a weak smile, Madison couldn't reply. Between being exhausted, irate, sullen, and embarrassed, she took several deep breaths, determined to keep from overreacting.

Her gaze drifted down to her skirt. She imagined cupping her hands around her mouth, shouting into it like a megaphone. "Yoo-hoo? Badass kung-fu skills? Are you up in there somewhere? No? Okay. Just checking."

Dammit. I hate when attractive, condescending men are right.

Barely traveling two blocks to her building, Fife was already slowing down to drop her off. "Have a good night, Ms. Taylor."

It was only then, as Fife wished her a good night, that she began to wonder.

How, in a company with tens of thousands of employees, did Alex Drake know my name?

FRUSTRATED, Alex sat in his private garage, the unrelenting pulse pounding through his body not letting him leave. He sat in his car, considering his second unbelievably terrible encounter with the beautiful Ms. Taylor.

"Madison," he said, correcting himself under his breath.

Inadvertently, he'd won a battle he hadn't meant to enter. But did he lose the war? Hurting her was never his intention.

Still primed from the scuffle on the street, his fight-or-fight-harder instincts kicked into high gear, refusing to be contained.

Lyft, my ass. Is she out of her goddamn mind?

The mere mention of a Lyft shot him to a new, uncontrollable level of totally losing his shit.

What the fuck was she thinking? If she'd hopped into a Lyft, how the hell would he know if she got home safely? And sending a dozen off-the-clock operatives in pursuit would be crazy. *Right?*

Clear as day, he saw himself, pacing all goddamn night like a keyed-up prom dad.

Let her think I'm an asshole. Join the club. It's for her own good.

The fresh thought of that man's hands on her had his mind spinning. *She needs protection.*

With the unrelenting pounding in his ears, he prepared for the worst, slumping into the soft leather seat of his Rolls-Royce Phantom. He didn't bother trying to start it. His trembling hand stopped him cold. For the moment, driving was a lost cause.

Motionless, he sat in the empty, silent garage. There was nothing to do but brace for impact. Ride it out.

As usual, the numbness washed over him. Then the cold. At some point, the trembling would ebb. He wiped his eyes and rubbed his face, dragging his fingers anxiously through his hair.

Painfully, a sentence echoed in a growing loop through his head, but he couldn't—*wouldn't*—bring himself to finish it.

If anything happened to her . . .

CHAPTER 7

MADISON

The next day, wearing office-ready slacks and carrying pepper spray in a pink lipstick-style canister, Madison headed to DGI—on foot—determined not to be afraid of her own shadow.

On the way in, she grabbed two egg-swiss-and-turkey-bacon croissants from the local deli, ready to share one with Joe. If the other didn't get eaten for breakfast, it would be fine for lunch. Nerves always wreaked havoc on her appetite.

But as she neared the towering headquarters, panic swept her to a run. Security guards were now prominently posted at each end of the building. Armed guards.

Where's Joe?

Within a few steps, she relaxed. Hidden at first behind the massive stature of a *don't fuck with me* security guard, Joe was propped up against the side of the building where he usually was. Filled with relief, she caught her breath.

Smiling, Joe looked up. "There's my Supergirl."

If only. "And there's my G.I. Joe. Here."

He took the warm sandwich she handed him, tucking it carefully into the pocket of his raggedy BDU jacket.

Worried, Madison squatted next to him. "Not hungry?"

Is he injured?

"AJ got me one earlier, but I'll save this one for lunch." He gave his pocket a few light pats, happy with his prize.

Madison exchanged a smile with Joe, then headed into the building. Thoughts of Alex Drake filled her head, like they'd done for most of her sleepless night.

Well, Mr. Drake, you might flaunt that asshole armor, but there's a knight in there. Somewhere.

Cheerful, she stepped up to the security desk. "Good morning, Fife."

"Good morning, Ms. Taylor. Hey . . ." He motioned for her to lean in, and Madison did, ready to receive a discreet message. "The boss wants to see you. He's in conference room 214."

Unsettled, Madison winced. *I'm so fired.* With a helpless look, she thanked Fife.

Well, it was nice while it lasted.

Apprehensive, she made her way to the second floor. Most of the meeting rooms in the building were glass walled, where anyone could see the goings-on. But room 214 was private, with a multitude of entrances.

Because DGI often hosted meetings where the confidentiality of the participants was highly prized, keeping their comings and goings under wraps was of the utmost importance. With an abundance of rumors and conspiracy theories, employees often speculated who visited, as well as how they came and went.

Rumors of hidden exits that led to other buildings popped up in whispered water-cooler conversations, and speculation about an extensive tunnel system sometimes crept in, perhaps leading to the White House. Or Area 51.

Finding the door slightly open, Madison peeked inside before mustering the courage to knock. Half seated on the edge of the massive cherry conference table was a man too gorgeous for words. She gawked in pure appreciation. It wasn't until he checked his watch that she snapped out of it.

With a hard swallow against the dryness in her throat, she laid a few light knocks on the oversized door.

"Come in."

The boom of his voice shot across the room, sending her pulse into a tizzy as she struggled for air. The frenzy of nerves in her stomach meant that breakfast croissant might not be eaten until dinner.

Entering, she found the room flooded with a comfortable brightness. The blinds were closed, but light glowed through the sheer shades.

Alex's face was rugged. Chiseled. And his bright eyes shined in this light. The lines of his face showcased a life of raw reality, amplifying a sexy-as-hell bad-boy presence mildly tamed by the soft lines of his custom-tailored suit.

Anxious, Madison stopped just inside the doorway, too shy to move, remaining at the perfect distance to admire every inch of the hot package known as Alex Drake.

Well, if this is the end, I guess there are worse ways to go.

Alex stood, but instead of buttoning his blazer in the customary fashion, he removed it.

Why is he taking off his jacket?

"Ms. Taylor, come in and close the door."

His jacket is off, and now I'm coming in and closing the door? To be clear, I don't have enough money on me for a lap dance.

Slowly, she complied, but kept her gaze locked on Alex as she did. He rolled up his sleeves, revealing just the tease of his muscles.

"Y-you wanted to see me?" Her voice cracked slightly, part fear of being fired, and part stammering like a front-row fan at a rock concert.

He gave her a quick once-over, and her breath hitched. Expressionless, he crossed his arms. "Well, I can see by your sensible sneakers that you opted to walk to work. Tough as nails, huh?"

She took the taunt, but after a night to think it through, she had a few choice things to say. And in her mind, it was now or never.

"Mr. Drake, I just need to say something." Uneasy, she let out a slow breath. "I apologize for not being more gracious about your offer yesterday. You were right. I was impulsive, and though what happened certainly wasn't my intention, I did end up putting myself, this company, and you in a precarious position. And for that, I am truly sorry."

He took a minute, eyeing her as he seemed to ponder her apology. Finally, he replied with a, "Hmm."

Did he say *hmm*? Or *mmm*?

Wait, why would he say mmm?

Allowing his lips to relax into a soft grin, he said, "But it's not going to change your behavior, is it?"

The question seemed innocent enough, but trick questions always do.

Its seriousness weighed on her. If she said it wouldn't change her behavior, she could be fired for something buried deep within the DGI personnel manual, some mention that under no circumstances could an employee ever put DGI in any form of risk.

On the other hand, if she conceded, assuring him that her behavior would change, well, it would be an outright lie. And Madison Taylor was no liar. Mostly because she was atrocious at it.

Cautiously, she said, "I'm not going to be a captive of my own fear, if that's the question."

Something in the glint in his eye and the widening of his smile calmed her. Like, he got it. *Could he possibly relate?*

"Let me tell you what I think, Ms. Taylor."

Madison braced for impact, gripping the back of a conference chair for support. Her eyes widened as he headed toward her.

"I've been replaying what I saw yesterday, and something about it is really bugging me."

Another step closer, and he was barely an arm's length away. "May I?" he asked, eyeing her arm. His intention remained unclear.

Unsure what she should do, she extended her arm, holding his attention, prepared for a handshake.

In a sweep, his hand wrapped firmly around her forearm, and she gasped in surprise. His playful eyes met hers, but he didn't release her. And she wasn't trying to get away. Patiently, she let him hold her, and his touch sent a tingle straight to the very center of her core.

"When you pulled away yesterday, you were wearing a very flimsy blouse."

Indignant, Madison rebuffed whatever the hell it was he was suggesting. "I didn't invite him to grab me, if that's what you're getting at."

Struggling, she tried pulling her arm back, but it was hopelessly locked in the strength of his immovable grip.

"No, what I mean is the fabric wasn't very, um, substantial. If you really had broken away from him, his hand would have closed, and he'd be left clutching your blouse. It would have torn by the time your arm swung into my chest. See?"

He demonstrated with her blouse sleeve.

She caught on, nodding as the epiphany hit her. "He let me go."

Alex nodded back, seemingly satisfied that she understood. "He let you go. He used the momentum of your pull to push your arm into my chest."

With that, he pulled her arm into his chest, replaying the events of the day before. She couldn't help but notice the mass of solid muscles concealed beneath his pressed white shirt.

Yesterday, she hadn't noticed, too engulfed in the dangers of the moment. But today was a whole new story, and her all-consuming awareness kept her arm absolutely glued to him. *Big-time.*

Indifferent to her schoolgirl gawking, Alex proceeded with his impromptu lecture. "Whenever you're in a situation like that, and hopefully you'll never be again, you need to take a moment and look at his hand."

Exaggerating his demonstration, he displayed his hand. It drew attention to more than his lesson. Despite his pristine manicure, his hands were marked by rough, faded scars that trailed up his arms.

What would have caused that? She peered shyly at his face. Were they the superficial evidence of much deeper damage?

Her gaze focused on his lips. While she'd been dreamy-eyed and curious, he'd apparently been talking the entire time.

"Focus," she heard him say, "on the thumb. That's your escape strategy. You're going to reverse karate-chop out through there in one quick motion . . ." He prodded her to try it.

Without overthinking it, she did, quickly freeing her arm. Pleased, she stood taller.

Again, he wrapped his hand around her arm, methodically bringing in one finger at a time, then firming his grip. Checking in with her, he asked, "Is that too tight?"

"N-no, it's fine." *God, it's more than fine.*

Madison breathed through the warmth rushing up her neck and face. Something about this very hands-on lesson was taking a turn for the naughty, but she wasn't about to admit it.

Jesus, this isn't a date, Madison. He's taking time out from his insanely busy schedule to not fire you and possibly save your life. Focus.

Reining in her mental bad behavior, she followed his words.

"Now, try." His tone was encouraging, and his eyes softened as he spoke.

Confident, she tugged a little toward the thumb-exit he'd pointed out, but nothing.

She sucked in a breath and tried harder. Then much less politely. No dice.

With a ridiculous amount of bravado, she really struggled to set herself free, playfully popping her foot up to nearly touch his thigh for a second—pantomiming her Oscar-worthy act of making a significant effort.

She caught his chuckle. Who wouldn't be amused? She was a teensy little sprite, trying to wrestle out of the hold of a smoking-hot giant.

Alex feigned a yawn while effortlessly maintaining his grip.

She gave up with an admission of defeat. "Okay, okay . . . I can't get away."

"Right. And with a behemoth like that guy yesterday, if he wanted to keep you held, he'd still have you in his grubby talons. So, you're going to do something unexpected that won't take much strength. Not that you're not strong, but your aggressor will probably be stronger. A lot stronger. So, you're going to block your natural tendencies to pull away, and surprise him with a swift little move that should put him on the ground. Ready?"

"Ready," she lied, her response coming out more like a question. Unconvinced, she really couldn't imagine escaping from such a strong grasp.

Not that I'm complaining. She softly sucked in a breath and bit the corner of her lower lip.

Alex paused, glancing at her mouth and then her heated cheeks before he continued. "Okay, I've got you. You're going to put your free hand on top of mine, forcing my hand to stay there."

She watched closely, then did as he directed. As Alex monitored her technique, she stole a few glimpses of his face, studying his tough and uncommonly striking features.

The urban legends about his allure over women are 150 percent true.

He nodded with approval, forcing Madison to squelch a giggle. He was approving her technique, not her musings. But she half supposed that if she dared to say it aloud, he'd probably nod just the same.

"Now, swing your arm around, and back-grab my wrist with your captured hand. Think of it as a variation of *wax on*, but where you end up having both hands grabbing him, and his arm and body will pivot involuntarily. It's a reflex. You then use the leverage of your position to force him to the ground."

Methodically, he walked her through the moves in slow motion, drawing Madison in. She noticed more than the complexity and effectiveness of each move.

Alex Drake's not just a guy with cool fighting skills. He's had some serious tactical training. He might have even taught it.

Captivated, she welcomed the tenderness of his tone and patience of his teaching. It all played out like a lesson Jack might have given her. If he were still here. In the oddest way, Alex reminded her of Jack, and she suddenly really missed her brother.

Pulling herself together, she concentrated, following the leader through a series of complicated steps. With very mild adjustments, Alex guided her as she moved through the technique.

Then out of nowhere, it clicked. *I've got it.*

Working through the move slowly at first, she thrilled as her confidence built. She whipped through it a little faster and more forcefully, instantly swinging his body and contorting it to the floor.

"Okay, okay, I give!" he shouted playfully.

Delighted at her success, she couldn't help the giddy squeal that escaped her throat.

Alex returned to his feet, giving her a disapproving glance that clearly said, *God, you're such a girl.*

Eager to please, she wiped her face of everything but pure

stoic professionalism. "Yes, I think I understand now. Thank you, Mr. Drake."

Her sudden shift to a serious demeanor drew a belly laugh from Alex. His dancing gaze darted met hers, and he closed the distance between them.

Her heart skipped a beat as she melted under his stare, sure that if she played poker with the man, every move she made would quickly give her away.

CHAPTER 8

ALEX

Alex Drake always had the amazing wherewithal to be good at practically anything. Whether engaging in major corporate wheeling and dealing or simply playing a hand of Texas Hold 'em, he was a natural, due in part to his uncanny ability to read people.

For years, he'd honed his nonverbal communication skills, knowing it would pay off, and it gave him the upper hand in almost any situation. But today, his usual advantage was crumbling under the sweet suggestive bits of his very own kryptonite.

With a laundry list of silent tells, Madison was his, and his will to resist was evaporating. He was all too ready to let go. Open his world. Unlock his heart.

But why?

He'd been approached by countless women over the years. Overtly, sometimes demanding, in the way one-night stands tended to be. But this . . . well, this was something entirely different. Irresistible. New.

Between the rapid pulse in Madison's wrist and the dilation of her pupils, her attraction to him was transparent. Compounded by the increased fullness of her lips as she slowly sucked in the lower one before biting it, he found himself fighting an internal tug-of-war he was willing to lose.

Between defending her and desiring her, he was dangerously close to falling for a woman he barely knew—and falling hard. So Alex concentrated, desperate to stay focused.

"Good. You're free. What do you do now?" he asked. Realizing he was a little too close, he summoned all his strength, keeping himself a safe few inches from her magnetic pull.

God, her lips are so fucking kissable.

Interrupting his stare, Madison stammered. "I . . . I . . ."

"Yes, Ms. Taylor?" His tone softened, and his eyes captured hers.

"I . . ." Her focus fell to his lips, and she licked hers ever so slightly.

What I wouldn't give for just one taste.

Ready to take her into his arms and never let go, he kept his voice low. "Go on."

Tenderly, he looked down at her, willing to lose all control. *What is it about her? Something different? Familiar?*

The electricity between them sparked with a connection that was undeniably real. Tangible.

Fighting the insane need to take her in his arms, he tamped down his desires and listened with the patience of a saint.

If I push her, I might lose her.

Despite the unrelenting attraction to her magnetic curves, her next words definitely got his attention.

"I, um, guess I'd kick him in the balls?"

At those words, his body instinctively tensed. Despite his captivation with her, just the thought of being on the receiving end of that move was the wake-up call he needed to free him from her allure.

Why are the prettiest ones always so evil?

Deliberately, he took a step back and rolled his sleeves down. Clearing his throat, he put his blazer back on.

"Not a bad suggestion, but not your best option." Still turned away from her, he buttoned his suit jacket, taking a few seconds to regain his composure. "No, Ms. Taylor, your best option is to use those stylish Brooks for their intended purpose." Turning back, he gave her a stern warning. "Get as far away from your assailant as possible."

Nodding, she boldly stepped toward him, and he welcomed her with a grin. "That's probably a good idea. I'd only kick him in the balls if I had my badass kung-fu skills with me."

Her teasing smile reminded him that he owed her an apology.

"Look, about that. I'm sorry for what I said. You didn't do anything wrong. I was just upset, but I was wrong to take it out on you."

"No need to apologize. I mean, you were right, after all." Madison's smile transformed as her eyes widened. "You were *right.*"

Her lips say I was right, but her eyes say she wants to kick me in the balls. It's a trap.

Ready to hand over a bigger apology, he sucked in a breath, prepared for full-on grovel mode. And maybe dinner. He'd do anything to get that beautiful smile back on her face.

Before he could speak, she cut in.

"You know, I'm probably not the only woman—or person, for that matter—in this multibillion-dollar company who doesn't know how to defend themselves."

"Yes. So?"

"So, sixty percent of our revenue comes from national defense, and not just our nation's, while twenty-five-percent of our work is in active contingency areas. All of our buildings have full gyms with training rooms that are barely used, on top of which we have an aggressive military recruiting program."

"All true." Not quite connecting the dots, Alex stood, riveted by her knowledge of his company. Madison hadn't been there that long, barely a month, but seemed to be a walking DGI encyclopedia, rattling off information like she'd majored in the subject.

And just when I didn't think she could get any sexier.

"Well, what if employees with these unique skills volunteered their time to teach varying levels of self-defense or martial arts, or both? It reinforces the image of a strong company that's also focused on employee protection and support. This would give us a recruiting advantage, and a public image that says strong companies start with a strong workforce."

Alex looked at her one last time, staring deeply as if he could see straight to her soul. Her shudder was nearly invisible, but it kept a satisfied smile on his face. There she was, giving him full witness to all the vulnerabilities she masked.

She's not just beauty and balls after all. She's got brains too. I'm going to marry this girl.

Strolling past her but keeping his eyes forward, Alex opted to hide his insistent desire to whisk her into his arms. Instead, he opened the door.

Madison couldn't take much more of Alex's darkening gaze but she stayed put, desperate to show her strength . . . and hide her shiver.

Decidedly, he looked away.

Again, he looks away? What would it be like to let go and lose myself in his strong arms and dark eyes?

Bitterly cold, he walked past her, avoiding her eyes at all costs, but damn near scorching her with his hot body so close.

Did I upset him? Maybe threatening to kick him in the balls was crossing the line.

Watching him walk away was disappointing and disheartening, but glorious all the same.

Alex opened the door but didn't turn back. His voice

commanding, he left her with a few parting words. "Make it happen, Ms. Taylor."

As the sound of his footsteps retreated down the hall, Madison broke out in a little happy dance. Rocking her moves with a hushed *yes, yes, yes*, she froze when her quirky twirl in place made her worst nightmares come true.

In the doorway, a small crowd was gathered, eagerly awaiting their use of the conference room. They seemed to enjoy her impromptu audition, filling the room with a chorus of *awws* as she cut her performance short.

Scrunching her face, Madison forced a grin, masking the heat of her cheeks as she pushed her way through the applauding group.

CHAPTER 9

ALEX

Calming the elated pep in his step, Alex entered his executive floor conference room.

Attentively, Paco and a small team sat up straighter in their seats upon his arrival. Leather-bound folders were perfectly positioned in front of every chair, providing detailed plans and a full itinerary for Alex's twenty-eight-day corporate trot across the globe, starting way before sunrise the next Monday.

Alex made himself comfortable at the head of the table, unable to erase the giddy smile pasted on his face, or evade the observation of Paco's amused eye.

Focusing on the work ahead, Alex opened the binder, a cue to his chief operating officer that he might proceed.

"Fourteen countries in twenty-eight days?" Dana said. "Just verifying you're good with that."

"Actually . . ." Alex flipped through the first few pages, scanning the itinerary for a small opportunity.

I need a day. No, two.

Unable to find an opening, Alex did what he does best. He made the opportunity he needed. "I'm not. Add Paris and Milan, in that order."

"Yes, sir," a senior analyst responded, quickly scribbling on his notepad. "Tack on two days to the end?"

Alex sped through the overview, rechecking himself. The last thing he needed was to make a long trip longer. "Yes," he said, more adamantly this time. Nodding, he clasped his hands. "Thirty days even. Sixteen countries with France and Italy added. That'll work. Now, let's walk through the strategies for each location."

As three enormous monitors lowered from the ceiling, dark but transparent blinds descended across the panoramic windows, still allowing views of the city's skyline. The monitors came to life, simulcasting the meeting to DGI offices around the world, with nearly two hundred executives hanging on the plans ahead.

Rick, the VP for global strategy, activated the presentation, ready to go through the massive report in exhaustive detail. "We'll start in South America, make our way across the Middle East to Asia, then ricochet back via Europe to meet key stakeholders. Locations and detailed agendas start on slide five."

With the presentation in full swing, Alex caught a text lighting up his phone. Not missing a word of Rick's report, he read and began a reply to the text as he asked, "Rick, I thought the Japanese were good with the initial plan. Why the extra day?"

"No change in the original deal," Rick said. "They requested a brief discussion on Project Venator on behalf of a major client. The meeting will tack four hours onto the next day but should prove quite lucrative. That, and they insistently requested a dinner the first night, as well as a presentation in your honor."

A shy grin showcased all the enthusiasm Alex would ever express, balancing his approval with humility. "Lucrative always works, and I appreciate their hospitality. I look forward to it. Please continue."

Rick did so, and Alex resumed a quick text tennis match with Paco.

PACO: Paris AND Milan? You're hardly the shopaholic. Business or pleasure?

ALEX: Business is always a pleasure.

PACO: You might be fluent in five languages, but votre français est merde. Très atroce. Perhaps you'll need a translator.

Alex pulled back his laugh to a stifled huff, conceding that his French, indeed, was not only atrocious, but complete, undeniable shit. Whatever. No matter how many languages Paco was fluent in, he still wasn't going on this trip.

ALEX: Hardly. Mandarin is the new language of money but won't be needed as both parties I'm meeting speak Italian. And with me out of the country for nearly a month, you'll be covering roughly 120 meetings.

PACO: Exactly 128, asshole.

ALEX: Hey, I'm not hitting Dubai, so it's not like you're missing the real shopping.

Avoiding more probes into his European detour, Alex set the phone facedown, determined to ignore any further texts or annoying glances from the Paco peanut gallery.

Alex looked up. In the lower right corner of the center screen, he found the page number of the slide presentation. *Eighteen. Of two hundred twelve.* Without a doubt, his ass would be planted in that chair for several more hours.

Giving in, Alex motioned the attendant for coffee.

CHAPTER 10

MADISON

One month later

Working at DGI was a dream come true, and Madison couldn't be happier. Well, not unless the sexy CEO who monopolized her dreams finally came around to sweeping her off her feet.

Grounding herself in reality, she blended seamlessly into the fabric of the tight-knit DGI team. Corporately, she excelled, which was as much of a shock to her as to anyone.

Trending analysis came easily to Madison, opening a surprising career path in a field that some might call monotonous. Or outright boring. But she was good at it and loved unlocking new opportunities for DGI's global expansion.

Her insights were strong, coming from a mixed bag of experience, natural intuitiveness, and an instinctive knack for understanding people.

And in a blink, that tiny spark of an idea for a small starter class on basic self-defense took off, exploding into full offerings twice a day, four days a week, with options in different techniques and skill levels.

In a company built by military veterans, it was easy to find a cadre of instructors willing to volunteer their time and eager to share their knowledge. The students were thankful, showering Madison with praise for such an amazing idea. But she took the success in stride.

No one's more grateful for a sense of purpose than this girl.

Keeping busy every second of every day filled a painful void in her life, and taking a beginner class or two helped. The instructors took her under their wing, flocking protectively to her side.

Their comradery gave her a few strong shoulders to lean on, but still, she wasn't eager to share. Grateful for the option, she opted to keep a small corner of her private life safely concealed. Yet without saying a word, they all approached her with caution and compassion. Deeply, they understood her loss.

Keeping busy had become Madison's coping technique, and she'd soon earned the solid reputation as a diligent workaholic. It afforded her a way to stay in the here and now, and away from the past.

And it was *almost* enough to keep Alex Drake out of her mind.

But every now and again, she couldn't resist rubbing her wrist, losing herself in the reverie of his hand wrapped around it. Of him. His strength. His smile. His scent.

So I sniffed the man. Who can blame me? It's not like I set out to catch a whiff of his tall, dark, CEO-ness. In my defense, he entered my airspace. And he smelled amazing.

He is amazing. And I'm just another dime-a-dozen analyst on his payroll.

Wake up, Madison—and smell the workweek.

Casually bumping into him in the hall might have been nice. Or perhaps in the lobby at the end of the day. With a slight pout, she once again decided cyber stalking was tempting, but out. If fate was on hiatus, so be it.

So, like most mornings, she started the day with piss and

vinegar, and a hearty plop into her soft leather chair. With a swift spin, she prepared to tackle another non-Alex-filled day.

As the dizzying spin of the chair slowed, she found an entirely new challenge to this particular workday. A little box from Tiffany & Co., placed neatly in the center of her desk, stared up at her with that seductive *come hither* look of that telltale robin's-egg blue.

She picked up the box with a giddy smile and then a suspicious glare. Studying it closely, she easily convinced herself the too-good-to-be-true offering couldn't possibly be what it seemed.

If Jack had taught her anything, it was to balance every new challenge with a strong amount of optimism and a healthy dose of skepticism. Squinting, she tipped the scales to full-blown doubt.

Unsure of what exactly to do with the little tease, she set it aside, leaving the pretty package on the corner of her desk. For the rest of the week, she worked around it, every so often allowing herself to curiously admire it.

A WEEK LATER, the swirl of her chair slowed to reveal another box had appeared. A big sister to the first.

Did someone add water?

As with the first precious box, Madison shied from temptation—no matter how much it tempted her with its glossy color and sexy black print.

With two outrageous desk ornaments neatly stacked, she now had a small pile going. Like some ultra-high-end Harry & David tower. Or an important piece of Andy Warhol pop art.

And if, by some miraculous stretch of the imagination, these really were from Tiffany & Co., leaving them untouched was of the utmost importance. After all, her patience seemed to be

paying off. A few more weeks, and her worst-case-scenario treasure trove would be sky high.

~

AFTER A FEW DAYS of smiling at the boxes only to have them
ridiculously tease her back, today Madison found a whole new
adventure waiting. Tented on her desk was a small note. No
envelope. With no markings on the outside.

It stood attentively next to the two boxes. With a curious
glance around, she unfolded it.

Aren't you going to open the boxes?

The boxes, like the note, had shown up first thing in the
morning, before she'd arrived. Which was really, really early.
Madison had been raised by a kind but crusty gunnery sergeant.
Bright and early was part of the package in the Taylor household.

Hardwired to work hard and learn harder, Madison was
usually the first in the building. More often than not, she beat
Fife in. Which meant that whoever the culprit was, they either
worked way too late or were insanely early.

Or sleeps here. Kudos to being one-upped by a fellow workaholic.

Madison also considered access to her office. With nothing of
value there, she never locked it. But every floor was highly
restricted, with each employee's access coded into their card. If
you didn't belong on a floor, you weren't getting there. Madison
worked on the fifty-first floor, just below the CEO and VP suites.

Despite its vast size, there were fewer than a dozen offices on
her floor, and only five had occupants. Three belonged to
women, one to a gay man who often carried on about his
wonderful husband, and hers. Two of the women had boyfriends
and the other was married. Systematically, Madison had elimi-
nated all the most obvious suspects.

Again, she read the note, studying the clean strokes of the uppercase handwriting as if it hid some clue. Gently, she bit her lower lip, thoroughly contemplating its suggestion.

If these boxes are really from Tiffany's, that means they probably contain incredibly expensive jewelry. That's sort of ridiculous. Sure, Tiffany jewelry just shows up. Because that's the kind of stuff that happens. All the time.

Taking the smallest box in her hand, she inspected it closely, then gave it a gentle shake near her ear.

It could be some sort of test? Or prank? A bizarre new form of corporate hazing. A camera likely waited to expose her. No matter what, this was most definitely not a small tower of diamonds. But maybe . . .

Snatching up her phone, Madison checked the internet. She tapped in the keywords *corporate*, *espionage*, *recruiting*, and *tactics*. Perplexed, she stared.

Seven hundred thousand results? Corporate espionage is going freaking viral.

Hurriedly, she scanned the results, one by one, leading her disapproving squint to end in a long nod. *This is exactly the type of tactic a corporate spy would employ.*

Deep in her search, she jumped at the startling ping of an alert on her desktop screen. The announcement of a new message nearly made her drop her phone. Catlike, she saved her phone from yet another screen crack, though nothing would save it from being distressed and outdated.

Carefully, she placed her phone on her desk, breathing out in relief. Crisis averted, she glanced at her monitor.

ANONYMOUS: Hi.

MADISON: Hi.

ANONYMOUS: I left you the boxes.

Flushed, Madison froze. *Oh my God, the corporate espionage recruiter is here in the building right now.*

ANONYMOUS: *I'm actually contacting you about some serious company business.*

Yup, here we go.

ANONYMOUS: *I'm taking an employee morale survey. What Starbucks beverage would make you happiest right now?*

Amused and smiling, she considered it. *Okay, not exactly the tactic I imagined. Actually, it's a hundred times dirtier. Luring me with Starbucks. Have you no shame?*

MADISON: *Right now? Well, in an effort to support employee morale, I'd have to say an iced matcha latte with almond milk.*

ANONYMOUS: *The green drink? Really?*

MADISON: *Hey, don't knock it. It's incredibly refreshing. My messenger app isn't quite identifying you. Who is this?*

ANONYMOUS: *Rather than just outright tell you, how about we meet? And if for any reason you're not interested, you go about your work and I'll go about mine. No questions asked.*

Madison's fingers lifted off the keyboard. *Should we meet?* When she took a bit too long to respond, Anonymous resumed typing.

ANONYMOUS: *Look, if I tell you who I am right off the bat, you might be less interested.*

MADISON: Really? Why?

*ANONYMOUS: Because I look like Igor and need to bribe
women with lavish gifts to spend time with me.*

Quietly, Madison laughed. His comment conjured memories
of a Halloween long ago. That year, her father had dressed as the
mad scientist; her brother, Jack, was Frankenstein's monster; and
Madison was relegated to be the lowly Igor.

Really? Igor? She'd be an amazing monster. She was born to
play the monster. Ask anyone. But Jack was eight years older.
And taller. His selection was obvious.

But Jack could never bear her crying. Or her wrath. So when
she absolutely refused to do Halloween that year, her brother
found a solution like he always did, and this one was perfect.

He'd be the monster for the first part of trick-or-treating, and
they'd switch during the second half.

Willingly, he'd assumed the role of Igor, delighting her as he
propped her high on his shoulders. To everyone, he introduced
her as Frankie. In turn, she introduced him as her loyal servant,
Igz.

For years, the nicknames stuck. Whenever someone had the
upper hand, that person would be declared Frankie, and the
other would be Igz.

Truth be known, Jack should have been the Frankie more
often than not, but he often carried the title of Igz. That was her
brother. Always giving her the upper hand. He did it so often that
Frankie became one of her steady family nicknames. In fact, her
dad still called her Frankie.

A sad smile lifted Madison's lips. Jack always took care of her,
and she really missed that about him. She missed him.

Realizing it had been a hot minute since she'd typed, Madison
postured her fingers to respond when another message beat her
to it.

ANONYMOUS: But my close friends call me Igz.

Stunned, she lost her breath. Dizzy and in disbelief, she reread the line.

Does he know?

How could he know?

There's no way this is a coincidence.

Espionage recruiter or not, she had to know exactly who this was.

MADISON: You don't have to bribe me with gifts. We can meet. Have coffee or something.

ANONYMOUS: I vote for "or something," but I guess a funny green drink will do.

Strangely, her smile returned, widened by his forwardness. Even with her anxiety in full swing, Madison was amused. Oddly charmed. But this round of anonymous speed-dating would have to wait.

Approaching footsteps pulled her back to reality. Work was beckoning.

Through the glass wall, she saw a uniformed deliveryman headed toward her office, a vendor keycard hanging from his lanyard.

MADISON: Hey, I've gotta run. Coffee sometime sounds great.

ANONYMOUS: Yes. Sometime soon.

The deliveryman peered in. "Madison Taylor?"

"Yes," she said, stylus in hand, ready for whatever required her signature.

Instead, he handed her a venti-sized clear plastic Starbucks

73

cup with a creamy green iced liquid inside. Taken aback, she had nothing but a blank stare for the deliveryman.

Quickly, he reassured her. "Don't worry. The tip was already covered. Enjoy, and have a great day!"

She whipped back to her computer screen to find Mr. Anonymous was offline. She didn't have a chance to thank the charming spy.

A little deflated, she did what any girl in her position would do. Smiling, she wrapped her lips around the straw, sucking in a slow sip of the scrumptious drink. The flavor instantly set her at ease, and let out a little hum of delight.

Corporate spy or not, until I know for sure, next time I'm telling him I also like paninis.

CHAPTER 11

MADISON

Days later, Madison was still distracted, fixated on the last messages from her virtual pen pal. Likewise, the little blue boxes continued to taunt her. There they sat, constantly reminding her of her anonymous admirer, and their anonymous small talk, followed by a deliciously anonymous drink.

But even as Friday came and went, Mr. Anonymous hadn't returned. Poof. Gone.

What exactly would that missing person poster look like?

All weekend long, Madison spent the time between chores and romance novels wondering about her mysterious friend. But as the days became a week, then two weeks, she'd had enough. Back at work, those sexy blue boxes double-dog-dared her to get to the bottom of it.

Game on.

Thinking he might have given her an accidental clue during their dialogue, Madison dusted off her best detective skills. She started by striking up conversations with random employees entering the break room, beginning with what she considered to be her most likely lead.

First, she asked about the morale committee. Was there one? And if so, who ran it? The responses ranged.

Some said, "Morale committee? What a great idea." Others came back with, "We're paid too much to need morale." And then there was the "Like I need one more bullshit thing wasting my time. Additional duties as assigned, my ass."

The only real conversation she got was from some guy buried behind an international copy of the *Wall Street Journal*. As soon as she asked about the morale committee, he carried on and on, brimming with enthusiasm . . . entirely in Chinese.

Flustered, she needed a new tactic. Thank God the man never popped his head up from behind the paper. He would have gotten a good look at Madison's frustrated eye roll at yet another dead end.

When his ramblings subsided, she meekly but politely excused herself, thanking him shyly with *sheh-sheh*—the only Chinese she knew.

Redirecting her investigation meant a new strategy. Next stop? The IT department. The super-geeky and ultra-friendly techie twins were always up for a challenge, and a possible favor.

The tech guys were apparently called twins because they look eerily similar, with the same 1960s NASA engineer glasses and button-up, short-sleeve shirts. Although, by age, they could easily be father and son.

Their side-by-side rolling chairs only added to their singular persona. Playing to the hype, they shared one nameplate with "TRex" prominently displayed on it. The term was a hybrid of Ted and Rex, their actual names.

When Madison explained what she needed, Ted volunteered their services on behalf of himself and Rex. "We can help!"

With a not-so-subtle glance shared between them, they seemed to be hatching an idea. By their expressions, it had to be diabolical.

Rubbing his hands together with sinister glee, Rex said, "For the right price."

As if on cue, Ted rolled his chair to a wall cabinet and pulled open a middle drawer. Rex just smiled.

If he pulls out a metallic bikini and Princess Leia hair buns, I'm out of here.

Instead, he grabbed a glossy sheet of paper and unfolded it before handing it to her. Glancing at it, Madison was surprised and relieved to see it was a Girl Scout cookie order sheet.

"We're not supposed to have this out, but my daughter can really use some sales, if you don't mind."

Eagerly, Madison perused the list. It hadn't changed much since she used to sell these little gems. Committing to a box of Thin Mints, she handed over a ten and the cookies were hers.

The box didn't stand a chance. Before Ted could give her change, Madison had the box popped, a sleeve torn open, and two cookies shoved in her mouth.

The men just stared.

"Sorry, I haven't had lunch," she mumbled through a mouth full of cookie.

By their wide-eyed gaze, she could see herself through their eyes. The *nom-nom-nom* sounds escaping her overflowing mouth, with cookie crumbs flying everywhere. Cookie Monster Madison in all her glory.

When she offered the open end of the sleeve to the fellas, they pounced with appreciation for a mid-afternoon snack.

Pointing a cookie at her, Rex piped up. "We're just glad to see a girl eat. We've heard rumors that your kind stopped doing that."

"Not this girl," Madison said, flipping another cookie into her mouth like a chip.

Snacked up and raring to go, TRex let Madison know that an anonymous message account was totally possible.

Yes, that's the sort of smoking-gun tidbit that brought me here.

And there were only a handful of ways one could do it from within the DGI firewalls.

Ted offered more. "They'd have to be either a guest user or a privileged user. Guest users are rare for us. We don't like outsiders on our networks. Privileged users . . . well, there might be a few dozen."

Now we're getting somewhere.

"We're happy to look into it, but . . ."

"But?"

Rex shrugged. "Well, as soon as we figure out who they are, we have to report it. It's technically grounds for immediate termination."

Immediate termination? Well, hell, I don't want to get anyone fired. I mean, what if it's not espionage? What if he's just really, I don't know, shy?

Covering her tracks, Madison played it off as research. For a course she was thinking about taking. Apparently, that was nerd code for a barrage of questions and free tutoring offers.

Without actually naming a school, professor, major, or course, Madison skated through their friendly interrogation and avoided more questions by flipping the script.

"Hey, is there a volume discount on the cookies?"

She must have hit the right note, because Ted's eyes lit up enthusiastically as he followed the smell of money. With her order placed, he explained that he only kept a minimum inventory onsite to satiate the usually predictable level of demand. He handed her the only remaining box and promised to deliver the rest in a few days.

Cookie booty in hand, Madison hightailed it back to her office. Realizing she'd wasted her entire lunch break chasing a phantom, she fended off any hangry tendencies by allowing herself just one more cookie.

Decidedly, she kicked off her heels, halting the investigation for the time being, and forced her focus back to work.

A few shakes of her mouse refreshed her screen. Staring once again at the unchanged messenger window, she couldn't help but wonder if there was a genuine reason he hadn't chatted back.

What if something happened? Maybe . . . he was caught? Possibly fired? Jailed?

After a sigh and blank stare at her screen, her wondering was rewarded.

ANONYMOUS: How was your drink?

Unintentionally, Madison beamed. *He's back. Totally not incarcerated.* If Mr. Anonymous was a privileged user, there's no way he'd be recruiting a new analyst for some extreme corporate spy game.

Smiling, she revved up for round two.

MADISON: Amazingly refreshing. Thanks. You certainly know how to make an impact.

ANONYMOUS: You wouldn't open those two little blue boxes brimming with potential, so I figured I'd better step up my game. Buy a girl a drink. With that out of the way, are you ready for "something else"?

MADISON: Something else? Wow, you must be the president of the morale committee.

ANONYMOUS: I do what I can.

MADISON: So, you're back?

ANONYMOUS: Yes. I didn't mean to disappear on you. A few things came up out of town. If it's any consolation, I had no fun at all.

MADISON: Two weeks and no fun? Sounds like you're the one who needs the gifts.

ANONYMOUS: Who needs gifts when I'm looking forward to "something else"?

His casual banter drew her in. Despite her aversion to office romances, she couldn't help it. He was funny and sweet, with enough of an edge that she was dying to find out who he was.

But one bad date, and work could become a perpetual land mine of awkward situations.

Been there. Done that. Got the T-shirt.

She held back a response, relieved to see Mr. Anonymous taking off the pressure by typing. A second later, she realized the pressure was just beginning.

ANONYMOUS: Hey, you know Gina?

MADISON: Tough-as-Nails Sawyer? Mr. Drake's VP of human capital?

ANONYMOUS: So, you know her. Great!

Maybe this was her in. *Come on. Throw me a bone.*

MADISON: Yes, I know Ms. Sawyer. How do you know her?

ANONYMOUS: Gina and I go waaay back. We've worked together for years.

Well, that wasn't much of a clue.

ANONYMOUS: Anyway, she'll have something for you late Friday afternoon.

MADISON: What is it? Should I call her?

Maybe this guy's in HR. Madison thought she'd signed all her onboarding paperwork, but it was possible in the hundred or so pages that she might have missed one signature.

ANONYMOUS: Nothing urgent, and it won't be there until Friday. She leaves at six that day, but she won't have it until after 5:30. Small window. Don't forget.

Smiling, Madison turned up the heat.

MADISON: I don't know.

ANONYMOUS: You don't know?

MADISON: I'm terribly forgetful. Remembering might be tough without a calendar invite. Mind shooting me one?

There are no anonymous calendar invites.

ANONYMOUS: I have a feeling you'll remember. Besides, if you know who I am, you'll never get out of your office and make friends.

Giggling and astonished, she pressed for more.

MADISON: You heard I was asking around?

ANONYMOUS: Maybe I did. Maybe I didn't. Maybe I caught you asking about me. Or maybe, just maybe, you asked me about me.

Thumbing through a mental picture book of everyone she'd spoken with, she kept her cool.

MADISON: *That's a lot of maybes.*

ANONYMOUS: *You covered a lot of ground.*

Stumped in this stalemate, she played one last card.

MADISON: *So . . . no hints?*

ANONYMOUS: *No hints. Need another green drink before I go?*

MADISON: *No thanks. Is "something else" off the table?*

ANONYMOUS: *Definitely not. Gotta run.*

He punctuated his statement with a little emoji running man. And again, Mr. Anonymous was gone.

Pouting, Madison scanned the calendar, noting with no surprise that today was Monday. She huffed in frustration. Without a doubt, the delicious anticipation meant sleep for the next few days was a lost cause.

CHAPTER 12

MADISON

By late Friday afternoon, Madison had completely lost track of the time, immersing herself in the quarterly market analysis report.

Simultaneously, both her computer and phone reminders pinged her. In the midst of an incomplete calculation, she decided that any more work on it would definitely wait.

Five thirty. Friday. Finally.

With a few keystrokes, she messaged Gina's assistant, requesting access to the executive floor. A few moments later, she received a confirmation her card was good to go.

The elevator doors opened as Madison arrived at the fifty-second floor. Seeing Madison through the glass wall, Gina stood, ready to greet her, a marked difference from their last encounter. Her assistant must have just left, but Gina waved her in.

"Good evening, Ms. Taylor."

Madison was usually the one on the service side of industry, so being addressed so formally by a superior threw her off.

"Please, call me Madison," she said as she handed Gina a box of cookies.

"Thanks, Madison. How much do I owe you?" Gina asked, pulling out her purse.

"Not a thing. Seriously, you're saving me from myself. I'm already a sleeve deep in these scrumptious goodies. And let's just say there's plenty more where those came from."

"Thanks, I'm starving. And there's something waiting for you through those doors." Gina didn't skip a beat, tearing into the box of cookies as her phone buzzed. She glanced at the text. "Shit, my wife's threatening to head to the restaurant without me. You can use the room to your heart's content. Pretty much everyone's gone."

Pretty much? "So, who's left?"

"Oh, I almost forgot." Gina grabbed a card from her desk, handing it to Madison with one hand while dialing her wife with the other. "Baby, I swear I'm on my way. No, I didn't eat," she fibbed after choking down a cookie.

And with that, Gina raced away.

Madison's chance to ask about the identity of her mystery admirer vanished. *Well, maybe this is the big reveal.* She pulled the note out of the envelope, her intrigue building.

I'm batting 2-0 on you opening boxes,
so I guess I'll go big or go home.
Try these on for size.

She headed through the door leading to some sort of washroom. But washroom definitely meant different things to different people.

Apparently, places that sold slushies and roller food had an entirely different type of restroom—the polar opposite of the fifty-second-floor executive lavatory. The space was an absolute palace, with an Italian leather chaise positioned in its center. With twenty-foot ceilings and skylights, the room was impressive and bright.

Mahogany walls were intermittently graced by floor-to-ceiling mirrors, giving Madison a head-to-toe eyeful of herself. A little intimidated, she smoothed her hair, trying to look less frazzled in the elegant space.

Looking around, she realized the toilets and sinks were down a small corridor, with private stalls enclosed by stately arched wooden doors. Tasteful gilded fixtures were abundant, giving an Old World touch to the room.

On a lavish chaise were two boxes. One was the size of a shoebox, and the other more suited for a garment.

Like a child on Christmas morning, Madison pounced on the largest, giving it a quick shake. Giddy, she tore the lid away, rummaging through the delicate layers of silver tissue. Inside was a stunning black lace dress that could have graced the cover of *Vogue*.

Whipping up the exquisite gown, she accidentally knocked the smaller box onto the floor. Panicked, she scooped it up, praying she hadn't broken something fragile or pricey.

Or worse, fragile AND pricey.

Carefully, she set it on the chaise. The box was intricately rigged with a hinged lid. When she opened it, a pair of shoes lifted out, spotlighted by an LED hidden in the lid. The stiletto heels were secured with a small tension groove.

"Oh," she said with a sigh. *They're beautiful.*

As Madison studied them like a curator inspecting fine art, her hand flew to her lips, covering her gasp. The resemblance was astonishing.

These were the shoes—*her* shoes—that had broken the day she was hired. She looked closer, realizing they weren't *her* shoes after all. These were much nicer—but were an identical replica of her old shoes.

Clearly, hers hadn't returned from the landfill, miraculously repaired. Those were goners. No matter how she'd hoped and prayed after pouring a hell of a lot of superglue on that heel, the break was final.

Ceremoniously, with thankful words and an ache of regret,

she'd thrown them away. Her beloved seven-year-old heels were so precious, they'd only seen the light of day a few times. And no matter how they cut into her heels and pinched her toes, they always looked new.

But now, in their place was a perfect brand-new pair, practically dancing the cha-cha in the spotlight. Oddly, the box and shoes were devoid of a brand name or logo.

Judging by the soles, this pair had never touched the ground. Enchanted with excitement and whimsy, she had to slip them on.

The fit was pure magic, more so because unlike her old pair, this one had the comfort of an Ugg slipper, caressing her foot like a cloud.

I guess that makes me Cinderella.

And as much as they worked with the suit she was wearing, her fairy godfather had a gown ready to go, one that beckoned her to try it on.

Here goes nothing.

Madison shed her corporate ensemble and pulled on the slinky gown with an overlayer of fine lace. The dainty fabric practically melted onto her skin and hugged every curve, making a bra impossible to pull off.

Promptly, she slipped off her bright pink bra and put the dress back on, watching the design fall into place. Though not usually one to linger over her reflection, she couldn't help it. The look was flawless.

Admiring the view, she smiled wide as her gaze worked its way up from the precious shoes to the sweeping cut of the beautiful gown.

Abruptly, the good vibes stopped at her face.

Oh my God, what's that?

She squinted, taking a closer look at her mouth. "Oh, you've got to be kidding."

Nothing says enchanté *like Thin Mint in the teeth.*

A knock at the door meant there'd be no digging it out at the moment.

Battling a mild panic attack, Madison held a hand to her racing heart as her anxiety ratcheted up to the stratosphere. Touching the door handle ever so slightly with the other hand, her fingers stalled. But the slight rattle of her hand on the lever was enough to give her position away. She heard a soft voice call out, the naturally deep tone soft and coaxing.

"Madison?"

It wasn't until that moment that she realized she'd been holding her breath. When his low voice called her name again, she exhaled, relaxing her tension even more. His deep voice was more than warm and relaxing—it was recognizable.

I know the man behind the curtain.

She slowly pulled open the heavy door, shyly peering through the space as it widened. His dark, majestic presence gazed down at her.

"Mr. Alex Drake, the great and powerful wizard of Igz?"

"Yours truly," he said, leaning his head against the door.

The moment stilled.

Taking her time, Madison reveled in his tender expression. The lines of his face were softer than she remembered, and his lips smiled with a charm that could melt panties from a mile away.

Calmly, she waited as his gaze swept over her before returning to her face. His eyes were dark and suggestive, piercing deep into her soul as he invited her to his.

She stood there, gawking at a man too delicious for words. Comfortable. Smiling. He had to feel it. The electricity between them.

God, I could lose myself in this man.

Madison couldn't help prolonging her stare, even as Alex broke the spell to check the time.

"Is everything okay?" he asked. "Are you still getting dressed? I was—" He glanced down, oddly staring a little too long at his watch as his facial expression twisted.

Her gaze swept down, then away as she smothered a giggle.

Yup. He definitely feels it.

She pretended not to notice as the tent in his slacks did its damnedest to make her acquaintance.

Rushed, Alex continued, and she met his eyes with her full attention. "Uh, I was going to show you something, but if you don't come out soon, we're going to miss it."

She ignored him as he casually pocketed his hands in a poor attempt at a magician's flip of the wrist. Apparently, dragging his Louisville slugger to an inconspicuous position would take a little more than sleight of hand.

Grateful that her gown concealed her own weeping core, she turned away. She'd imagined him a million times . . . from the isolation of her cold bed and her hot hand, but nothing prepared her for the reality of him.

The man standing here was handsome and funny, and bigger than life in more ways than just his package. With the warmth of his smile and the heat of his body, she was without a doubt going to be putty in those big, strong hands of his.

At least, a girl can hope.

Madison struggled for control of her face, not wanting to risk widening her smile. If she did, this gorgeous man would get a full view of her pearly whites rimmed in chocolate.

Straining, she kept her teeth hidden behind a wall of pursed lips. Any smile, no matter how small, would reveal all the signs of a well-crafted hobo disguise. Stubbornly, she pressed her lips together a little tighter.

He backed away with a frown. "You seem concerned. Is it because of our first encounter?"

Losing the war with her smile, she rushed to the corridor, eagerly finding the furthest sink. She called back, "No, of course not. You were incredible. You really saved me, and Joe."

"I mean the time before that."

Curious but preoccupied, Madison asked, "What time before that?" She peeked her head back from the hall. "Sorry, I just . . . I need a moment to freshen up. I'll be right back."

She knew her departure was abrupt, even rude, but leaving the tall, dark, and handsome CEO with the seductive scent couldn't be helped.

"I'll just be a second," she called out, hoping to reassure him enough to keep him from leaving.

As she ran the tap water and scooped some into her mouth for a swish, she barely made out his side of the conversation.

"Look, I know I kind of just sprang this on you, and if you're uncomfortable at all—"

His gallant ramblings to put her at ease were cut short by her quiet gargle, followed by the loudness of spitting in the sink.

Hmm, if he heard that, he's probably thinking that sound usually comes after a bit more intimacy.

Satisfied after a final check of her teeth, Madison returned to the waiting hunk. She blew out a breath, feeling much more relaxed.

With his blazer unbuttoned and his tie noticeably loosened, every bit of him seemed defeated. Maybe giving up on whatever he had planned.

"Sorry." She smiled wide and explained. "I had a small smudge of Thin Mint I needed to get off my teeth." She stepped closer. "I didn't quite hear you." Hopeful, she lifted her gaze to meet his.

Alex stood taller, towering over her with the solid body of the most attractive man she'd ever seen. His gaze might have been disarming, but the dimple that appeared with his boyish grin made her absolutely weak in the knees.

"Thin Mint, huh? Well, I think you may have missed a spot." The ball of his thumb gently rubbed the outer edge of her bottom lip, wiping what could only be an indiscernible smudge of chocolate from her mouth.

Madison held herself steady, giggling between smooth swipes, letting him finish. He followed the gesture with a ridiculously exaggerated display of diligently examining his thumb before sucking it ever-so-slightly clean.

God, that's hot.

He popped his brow, businesslike as he asked, "Who's your supplier?"

I can't rat out Ted.

"Oh, I've got friends in high places." Wide-eyed, she shocked even herself with the preposterousness of the comment, considering the man she was speaking to.

"Do you now?" Playful and knowing, his eyes lit up. "Then it *must* be Ted."

Frozen, Madison couldn't think of a word to say. Obviously, nothing happened at DGI that Alex Drake didn't know about. Timidly, she asked, "If you know, then why is he so secretive?"

"Because he sells a crap ton of cookies that way. Forbidden fruit and all. Seriously, he and his daughter outsell everyone else in the troop by three to one. Let's take you, for example. How many boxes did you buy?"

"Um, six . . ."

Both his eyebrows lifted high. "Six?"

". . . teen. Sixteen, actually, but he cut me a deal."

Alex gave her a spirited smirk. "Soon you'll be outbuying me."

"Well, I'm a sucker for a great deal and a good cause encased in mint-chocolatey goodness."

Exaggerating a sly shift of his eyes to the left, then the right, he leaned in. Confiding in a deep, authoritative tone, he shared a bit of wisdom. "Be leery of a Ted in sheep's clothing . . . and watch out for his poker game."

"Noted." Madison nodded, filing away for later the possibility of a future poker game.

Alex returned to the task at hand. Her heart raced at his insistence.

"Seriously, I need to know how to lure you out of here." He leaned closer, his lips nearly touching her ear as he whispered, "I could carry you on my shoulders, if you like."

Madison tempered her astonishment with intrigue. "That! That right there. What made you say that?"

Folding her arms, she kept them light and loose. *Is he guessing? Or does he know?*

He rebuttoned his blazer and displayed all the signs of a man ready to leave. Giving her a tender smile, he said, "Let's just say I've got friends in high places too."

Alex's tone was gentle and easy, and in a strange way, sentimental. It made her want to get to know so much more about him. Then his elbow leisurely winged out, inviting her to take it.

Instantly, her arms unlocked, and her hands couldn't help but wrap around the warmth of his arm. She enjoyed nestling her fingers in the inner crease of his elbow, clinging to the strength of his bulging bicep.

Leaning against him comfortably, she let him lead her out of the room, arm in arm. "The way I figure it," she said, "either you're a mind reader, or . . ."

"Or?" He slipped his warm hand over hers, melting her completely into submission.

Breathless, she took a second before continuing. "Or you've paid way too much to get information on me that's absolutely worthless. Possibly bribing all the moms in my hometown. Although they wouldn't need much enticing. Your smile and a bit of *pass the prosecco*, and those ladies would sing like the cast of *Mamma Mia.*"

"Well, now I feel like I've missed an opportunity. And information always has value," he said as they stopped at his office door. "I've built an empire recognizing that things others think are worthless might, in fact, be absolutely priceless . . . like this."

A warm rush spread across her neck and face as he seemed to

be leaning in for a kiss. Instead, he moved in to open the door, making way to his very dark office.

"Open blinds," he commanded.

As the blinds obeyed, the glow of a radiant setting sun filled the room, with glints of gold flashing here and there on every bit of glass and metal in the expansive room. The panoramic wall of windows showcased breathtaking views of the Manhattan skyline and Central Park below.

The honey-drenched sky captivated Madison until a curious glance around led her gaze straight to a familiar tower. The two Tiffany boxes patiently waiting on the oversize executive desk stared back, taunting her yet again.

Too easily, he peeled away from her grasp.

Spoilsport.

Alex grabbed the larger of the two boxes, bouncing its weight in his hand. It wasn't until that moment she considered it might actually be heavy with no-kidding diamonds ready to adorn her wrist.

With the box displayed in his open palm, he presented it to her.

Studying his eyes, she found the irresistible glint that sparkled all this time had lost its shimmer, and the grand gesture began to feel expectant and empty. For the first time since the pretty box appeared in her life, her interest in it waned.

I just want to get to know him.

After a moment of pondering, she reluctantly took it. Erring on the side of hope, she didn't open it. Instead, her fingernails tapped gently across the top of it as her gaze wandered to the wall of windows.

"You said something about the first time we met. How *do* we know each other?" she asked, half wondering if he was toying with her, like a cat might with a mouse before swallowing it whole.

"How about I make you a deal?"

Alex stepped closer behind her as he spoke, and his warm breath feathered over her cold shoulders, sparking a shiver. Her breathing hitched as his hot palms ran over her bare upper arms, warming them as he softly caressed.

He has to know what the heat of his body is doing to me.

"If it doesn't come to you after we've gotten to know each other better, I promise I'll tell you how we met. And tell you everything else."

The last word hung in the air after he finished. *What else is there?*

Madison whirled around and stepped back to more fully face him. The cold window against her back startled her, propelling her body right into his. Helplessly caught in his embrace, she silently cursed the lovely blue box still in her hands, now sand-wiched protectively between their chests.

"Well," she said, "you've gone to an awful lot of trouble. I mean, the dress. The shoes. Seems like a lot just to get to know a girl."

CHAPTER 13

ALEX

Alex relished the memory of doing all this. For her.

Madison's dress size was a breeze. In fact, estimating it from the video footage of her in Gina's office wasn't even necessary. The views of her curves from every angle were burned in his memory like a fresh branding.

Still, he watched the video more than once to reassure himself of her size. But the replay of her passionate moves relieved his stress a hundred times better than booze.

Some guys focused on sports stats, but Alex Drake was all about perfection and precision. And without a doubt, this girl was perfect. Madison Taylor was precisely a 36-C. By the jiggle, every bit of her voluptuous bosom was a full C, and borderline D.

The dress was his own design—a doodle he sketched out during the staff meeting from hell before his trip. The dainty little number was a sublime blend of Victoria's Secret meets Audrey Hepburn. Like Madison, the gown was elegant with a fiery, sexy edge. During his layover in Paris, an eager designer was just as captivated by the footage, and created a gown that molded to her like a second goddamn skin.

God, I want to tear it off her.

The shoes were a bit tougher, yet something in her expression when they broke told him they were important. After pulling the feed from the lobby, he shot the video to his on-call clothier. They analyzed it from every angle, then advised him that his chances were best with a referral to an Italian shoe designer.

With a frenzy of emails, around-the-clock phone calls, a can-do attitude and an obscene amount of cash, their existence was solidified. By his final stop in Milan, her ensemble was complete, culminating in the vision he now adored before him.

Alex gazed down at her and grinned. "It was no trouble at all. You're easy to please."

The sweet smile that unfurled on Madison's skeptical face conveyed every ounce of her disbelief as she tugged up the box still trapped between them. "And this? Unless this is some sort of memory jogger on how we met, let's get to know each other before you shower me with lavish gifts. Though the occasional matcha latte is definitely appreciated."

Accepting the gift's return, he took it to his desk. After replacing the box with its mini-me, he admired them for a moment before turning back to her.

Alex stayed put, perplexed but pleased. He needed a moment —and not just for the nagging bulge trying to burst free from his slacks. For the first time in, oh, ever, a woman wasn't after his money or status. And though clearly interested, she wasn't chasing him. Everything about Madison Taylor filled him with a caring protectiveness he'd never imagined.

A feeling he suspected would just continue to grow.

She faced him, her body limned with the amber paint of a setting sun that backlit her in an angelic glow. But somehow, even though haloed in the moment, he knew a fiery, seductive devil lay in wait below that innocent facade.

Nothing about this woman was naive or contrived. He knew it, and his cock knew it too.

This temptress will be the death of me.

Those soft curves and inviting smile of hers made him lose his damn mind. But this had to be different. *She* was different. With a determined vow he wasn't sure he could keep, he decided that nothing would be rushed with her. Everything had to be beautiful. Lasting. Immensely pleasurable.

All for her.

Intensely, Alex watched Madison, and she remained still, letting him run his gaze over her body. He hungered to satisfy her deepest desires.

Everything about her, here and now, was breathtaking, backdropped perfectly as the last rays of sunlight slowly disappeared beneath the horizon.

CHAPTER 14

MADISON

Under the heat of his dark gaze, Madison turned away to stare unseeing out the wall of glass. "So, Mr. Drake, is this what normally happens when you bring a woman to your executive suite?"

Swallowing her nerves, she realized that definitely sounded less suggestive in her head. But she let the question linger in the erotic pull between them.

Hey, it's not my fault. That smoldering hunk of man knew exactly what he was doing. Breathing on my neck. Rubbing my arms. Smelling crazy good.

Chilled, she shivered, hoping to hell Alex would come closer already.

She sensed more than heard him stalk toward her. His body was close, but he didn't touch her. He didn't have to. The heat of him burned through her from behind, soaking her core.

His words were low, rumbling gently over her. "Listen, Madison."

Alex combed his fingers through her hair, sliding her tresses forward, over her shoulder. His breath singed the now exposed sensitive nape of her neck, and she gasped. Massaging her skin, he spoke softly.

"You're right. I've had lots of women here, and I've given many of them gifts. But I've never chased them. They've all chased me. And when I wanted it over—and I *always* wanted it over—a small token softened the blow. They left happy, and I moved on. Until now." His hands slid down her arms to her wrists, where he wrapped them with a squeeze. "Until you."

Until me?

Alex dropped a tender kiss on her shoulder, and she found his restraint unsettling.

He's holding back.

Desperately, she wanted him. Needed him. Her body pressed back against his, and the boldness of her movement changed the gentleness of his kisses and his hold.

His lips were everywhere, nibbling her shoulders, strong against her neck, pillowy against her cheek. Saying so much, and yet nothing at all.

Madison ignored the battle playing out in her head. In case her mind didn't get the memo, the match was fixed.

I get it. This isn't just my boss. This is the CEO of the company. If this goes south, life could be hell. But, God, does this man feel good.

Seriously, it should be illegal to feel this good. He touches me, and it's like he knows me. Knows everything. What I'm thinking . . . feeling . . . needing. And, boy, am I needing.

The spark in her hoohah was about to blaze out of control, with Firefighter Alex's name written all over it.

She bit her lip, arched her back, and reached down to claw at his thick thigh like a leopard in heat. Her other hand reached back, fisting his hair and tugging his head closer. Not wanting to muddle her message with a mixed signal, her moves demanded whatever he held back.

Mind, lay low. Body is breaking all the rules and bracing for Alex Drake impact.

When she spun around, his lips descended on hers, invading her mouth as his tongue broke through in long licks and forced strokes. She breathed him in, stroking his tongue with hers before he stopped and pulled back slightly.

"Madison," he said low. "Are you sure? I don't know what it is about you, but I know that once I start—with you—I don't think I can stop. And I don't just mean tonight." His forehead rested on hers as he stole a soft kiss. "If you have any doubts at all, it's fine. I can back off. Take it slow. Anything you need. Just tell me."

Smiling her reassurance, Madison licked her lips, his taste still fresh on them. She looked up, seeing the doubt behind his dark eyes and tense brow.

Her lips brushed ever so softly over his as she whispered into his mouth, "I'm all in."

His kiss burned back, awakened with a rush that crushed against her lips. His strong hands teased her with a touch that trailed from her neck down the sensitive skin of her back.

Alex hesitated only for a moment before swiftly releasing her zipper, letting gravity drag the gown to pool at her feet.

She moaned with need, feeling his hands warm every curve as he controlled her. A maestro to her impulses, he was masterful in every touch, as if he'd handled her for years.

This man had never before held her, but in every touch, he knew her. Her body was rapturous, moving in tempo to his will. Every sensation was filled with something she'd never known. She trusted how he handled her. She trusted him.

A soft kiss pressed to her lips. "If anything displeases you, I have to know. Understand?"

There it was again. A darkness to Alex's eyes that seemed worried and protective.

"Yes." She heaved out a breath, coaxing his lips back to her mouth.

He cupped a breast, caressing its weight before his mouth made its way to it. His lips nibbled across it, licking her nipple to a firm peak before grazing it with his teeth. She gasped hard as he suckled it, burning it with the heat of his mouth.

Heavy, her head leaned back against the window as his tongue sliced a line down her, pebbling her skin as he reached her core.

Her body burned in his hands, falling against the coolness of the window behind her. A harsh gasp escaped her throat as his breath melted her.

Dropping to his knees, Alex nuzzled his face into her plump wetness, kissing and licking her through her panties. The slightest whimper escaped her lips as his mouth brushed the top of her thong. Taking the slight band in his teeth, he tugged it down.

His powerful hand scooped up her thigh, balancing it over his shoulder. She stroked his hair as he knelt before her, and savored how he seemed to revere her.

With a long lick, he buried his face in her wetness.

"Oh my God." Madison pulled in a breath, gripping his hair and willing herself to hold off the rush of an orgasm.

Smearing her juices up to her clit, his fingers circled it. Massaged it. Then he pulled back just long enough to meet her eyes with a smile.

"Not yet," he said softly.

"Not yet," she whispered, submitting to his sweet demand.

After a tender kiss to her swollen pussy, Alex stroked his fingers against her, hot as they worked back and forth. Again, that dangerous tongue made a long lick before forcing its way deep inside. Her gasp rose to a cry.

Deliberately, he pulled out, teasing her entrance with his fingers before shoving one in. He gave her a few glorious pumps, hitting her spot over and over before pulling away.

After a swipe to her clit, he wrapped his lips around it before plunging two fingers so far in, she struggled for air.

Grinding her hips and following his seductive direction, her body swayed. Dizzy, she could feel herself coming completely undone by him.

It was all too much. His touch. His lips. *And, my God, that tongue.* She climbed higher, straddling Alex's mouth as she rode the waves of ecstasy across his lips.

Her panted screams tore through the room while her body collapsed from the eruption. Her inner walls shuddered, crushing his fingers to a stop deep inside her.

Tenderly, he lapped her gently, laying tender kisses here and there as she floated down. Finally, his fingers slid free.

Careful and slow, he eased her leg down until her foot met the floor. Caving beneath the weight of pure ecstasy, her body made a heavy slide down the cool glass until he caught her, sweeping her into a cradle tight in his arms.

Her head fell into the crook of his neck, and she nuzzled him, savoring his closeness. Her lips left kiss after kiss against his skin.

Alex carried her to a soft leather sofa, laying her down before resting his blazer over her. Her body stretched into the warmth it provided.

"I have a blanket if you'd like one."

Dazed and happy, she bit the fullness of her lower lip as she smiled and shook her head.

He sat next to her, and she couldn't help reaching up to stroke the hard lines of his jaw. He pressed his lips to her palm. His fingers slid a few strands of hair away from her face, tucking them behind her ear.

"What about you?" Madison asked, barely able to lift her heavy lids.

"There'll be time," Alex said softly, assuring her as he stroked her cheek.

Closing her eyes for just a moment, every muscle in her body relaxed. She held tight to her smile as she drifted to sleep.

CHAPTER 15

PACO

Paco Robles always strolled into DGI with the swagger of a man without a care in the world, regardless of the weight he carried on his shoulders each and every day. At nearly midnight, with no one around, his swagger was for his own benefit. He'd earned that swagger the hard way and proudly flaunted it, even with nobody watching.

His confidence was derived from knowing where all the bodies were buried, a consequence of owning the shovel and doing the digging. He'd been Alex Drake's heavy for the better part of a decade. With Alex, Paco managed to elevate himself, devoting much of his free time to smoothing away any of his remaining rough edges. A whore to nice things, but not status, he could easily distinguish a fine champagne from a Napa knockoff, yet usually preferred a frosty mug of whatever was on tap.

Some days Paco felt like the right-hand man of a mob boss, and other times he just felt like the fucking cleanup crew for whatever shit landed in Alex Drake's lap.

Paco was well paid for his talents, with his greatest gift being his ability to become a chameleon. He could dress down and blend into a crowd, or easily charm a boardroom full of the most powerful CEOs in the world. He commanded center stage when required, but more often than not, remained cloaked in his power of invisibility.

Swift with his camera phone, and discreet with a wide array of covert surveillance equipment, he captured whatever he couldn't commit to memory, which didn't leave much.

With a background in street fighting and mixed martial arts, what Paco lacked in bulk he made up for in speed and precision force. And still, few knew anything at all about him.

Aside from Fife, Paco was the only other person whose keycard gained him entrance to the boss's personal elevator, office, and the great Alex Drake himself. As one of only three people with unfettered access to the entire building, Paco came and went as he pleased, wherever and whenever he wanted.

Gina knew his salary was off the books, with prompt cash-only payments every Monday. No records were kept, electronic or written. No one ever questioned any requests he made, and any asks were to be considered those of Alex Drake himself.

Tonight, Paco's task was easy enough, but it weighed heavy on his mind. Making his way to his office on the executive floor that he might as well consider home, he slipped past Alex's office with a contemplative glance at the door.

Entering the comfort of his own luxurious space, Paco relaxed. He'd made every square inch of the room a reflection of his life. Souvenirs from all over the world were strategically placed to amplify their significance and importance.

Dropping into the plush executive chair, he pressed a button, relaxing back as it fully reclined. He gave himself the leeway to close his eyes, but he wouldn't sleep.

Patiently, he waited.

CHAPTER 16

MADISON

Cool air drifted over Madison's skin, waking her in the darkness. Disoriented, she lifted her head to glance around.

Instantly, her hands slid up and down her body. She was naked, in an empty office with just the peek of a flame rolling in a fireplace she hadn't noticed earlier.

With a soft yawn and a stretch, she reached around the sofa, then down to the floor, finding the blazer that had slipped off. She pulled the coat to her face with a soft moan.

As she inhaled his scent, the sweet seduction of the night came back, overtaking her in a swirl of unbelievable sensations. Relaxing into a cozy replay, she was startled when a few sharp raps at the door pulled her from her dreamlike retreat.

Still groggy, she smiled, her heart beating faster as she whispered, "Alex."

Slowly, the door opened.

"Miss Madison?" a male Latino voice said softly.

That's not Alex.

Panicked, she watched the door open with wide eyes. *Crap.*

"Just a minute," she called out, trying desperately to remain calm.

In haste, she threw the blazer around her shoulders, slipping her arms into it and wrapping it around herself like a kimono. As the man entered, she hopped to her feet, suddenly realizing she was still in the stilettos. Somehow, they seemed a touch dressy paired with the oversized jacket.

"Sunrise lighting," he said, his voice smooth and commanding.

Worried, she wrapped the blazer a little tighter as the room began to glow.

The man stepped in. His face filled with a warm smile, giving way to friendly eyes that remained trained on hers. "I'm Paco Robles. I'm here to help you with anything you may need."

Deflating, Madison couldn't help a twinge of disappointment. The man was kind, professional, and completely unfazed to find a half-naked woman in Alex's office this early in the morning.

Methodically, he scanned the room, then headed straight toward the scene of the hot and heavy crime. Scooping up her gown, he took care to lay the delicate lace carefully over his arm. She breathed a quiet sigh. Thankfully, her panties had mysteriously vanished.

She couldn't read the change in his expression, but something on the desk caught his eye.

"Unopened?" he asked, motioning to the blue boxes still on the desk. "I don't blame you on the earrings, but you really need to look at this one before you decline."

Gently, he hung the gown over the back of the chair, freeing himself to take the larger box in both hands. Eager and smiling, he carried it to her, taking a seat on the sofa and patting the space next to him, inviting her to sit. Slowly, she did.

Mesmerized as he handled the box, she watched as his fingers moved like a magician showing off a spellbinding trick. Swiftly, he opened it, pouring the contents into one hand. Another box slipped out, in the same gorgeous blue, but velvety.

With just the right amount of ceremony, he held it before

them, lifting the hinged lid slowly. Her mouth fell open, releasing an embarrassingly loud gasp.

"My sentiments exactly," he said, nodding with reassurance. "Tiffany and Company, ten and a half carats of brilliant square-cut diamonds set in eighteen-karat white gold."

A second later, the tennis bracelet was out of the box and he clasped it around her wrist. Admiring the bling, he reached for her hands, squeezing them as he met her eyes. "Hey, if you don't want the earrings, can I have them?"

Madison couldn't help but giggle as she played along. "Absolutely. Why not? Diamonds for everyone."

Paco joined in, laughing as he popped to his feet and headed back to the desk. Instead of retrieving the other box, he walked past it and faced the wall.

"Are you in a time-out?" Madison asked.

"Working here? Every day of my life," he said, a jovial ring to his tone.

She watched as he swiped an access card across a panel she'd only just noticed. The wall opened to another room. "Sunrise lighting," he said again.

Fascinated, she watched the enormous room light up. She stepped closer, a crazy curious moth to this super-secret flame.

"Miss Madison, here is where you can get ready to start your day. Panoramic views of the city, and the lighting will adjust as the sun rises."

It was a bathroom, but some crazy luxe version with state-of-the-art fixtures and more space than her living room and kitchen combined. *Alex Drake must live here.*

"This is the shower," he said, "with room for you and seven of your closest friends. Three rainfall showerheads, eighteen settings with programming and music options. And if you want to take a ride on the wild side, you have your own personal waterfall."

As he said the word *waterfall*, a surge of water poured out from the wall above to the smooth stone floor below.

"Infinity bathtub, in case you prefer a soak. Over here is the toilet. If the lid is closed, it'll open as you approach. The controller is in the wall. Heated and cool seat options, and temperature and steam options for the bidet."

A vajayjay steam? That might be where I draw the line. Maybe.

"This is what I like to call the magic mirror."

Paco headed to a wall of mirrors and picked up a remote. He pointed to the center mirror and pressed a button. The center third of the mirror transformed into a television, set to the local news. He clicked it off.

"And whatever you need—dryer, lotion, perfume, makeup— just press this button on the remote, and it works like your phone. Speak into it, and whatever drawer it's in will pop open. An outfit will be waiting for you when you're done."

With that, he departed.

Madison couldn't quite process the amazing room and all its glory. A sliver of sunshine peeking over the horizon meant Saturday was definitely here. She wished Alex were too.

As she realized she *really, really* had to go, it suddenly occurred to her that her first priority was to quickly master the space-age console controlling the toilet.

CHAPTER 17

MADISON

After the single most amazing shower of her life, Madison was overcome with a sinking feeling deep in the pit of her stomach. The reality of the morning after.

Perhaps the party was over. Mr. Robles had to be Alex's charming cleanup crew.

Pushing past her disappointment, she made a determined effort to enjoy all this luxury while it lasted. Whisking the remote from the sleek stone counter, she shyly said, "Hairbrush . . . oh, and a dryer, please."

Instantly, the dryer came out from a panel behind the wall, while a drawer filled with ten different brushes opened from below.

Trusting the magic mirror to fulfill her every demand, she asked for lotion. Another panel opened, filled with creams and lotions plucked straight from Ulta. The same with the makeup and perfumes.

After going through her morning routine, now armored with the finest luxuries the mirror bestowed, she moved to the cute little number hanging behind the door.

As magically as he promised, Mr. Robles had an outfit waiting. They were the special sorts of goodies that only a jaunt through Barney's or Bergdorf's could provide.

The little summer dress was both classy and sexy, with built-in padding to avoid the need for a bra, and just the type of flowy skirt she loved. A delicate thong and a sweet little clutch were also part of the package.

Rounding out the look were a very unpractical pair of strappy heels that managed to make every pair of shoes she'd ever owned look like flip-flops. She read the labels of the shoes and purse, shocked.

Louboutin? And Hermès?

Even if she wanted to protest wearing all these unbelievably stunning clothes, she had no alternatives at the moment. And if this were the end of her Alex Drake story, these were a pretty remarkable stash of consolation prizes.

That being said, they were of little consolation. Sadly, the prize she coveted most slipped away in the night.

Madison glanced at the mirror one last time, ignoring her pout. Out of habit, she swept her hair behind one ear. Her naked earlobe made her wonder.

What was in the other box?

As soon as she stepped to the door, it opened. The rich aromas of bacon and coffee that met her nose gave her a whole new sense of purpose. A lavish breakfast was set up at the conference table, just waiting for her to dig in.

A loud grumble from her tummy reminded her that her dinner last night had consisted of a sleeve and a half of cookies for her main course, and Alex Drake for dessert. Real food was an absolute necessity.

But first, priorities. The little blue box on Alex's desk was calling her name. She reached over to pick it up, but found it slightly open. Peeking inside, she couldn't believe her eyes.

It was empty.

Madison glanced around, assuming the contents had

somehow spilled from the desk onto the floor, but her round of millionaire egg hunt turned up empty.

A familiar chime sent her on a new hunt, following the sound to find her phone. It sat next to an elegantly covered plate of food, with her purse from the night before lying behind it. The phone was compelling, but a second growl from her stomach assured her the message could wait.

She sat and removed the heavy lid. Hidden beneath was a beautiful buffet with yummy written all over it. The plate held two hard-boiled eggs, bacon, sausage, and a mini-croissant next to a small blueberry scone. A steaming pot of coffee sat next to a porcelain cup, flanked by crystal salt and pepper shakers, and a bottle each of chilled Voss still and sparkling water.

Moaning with bliss as she chomped on a crispy piece of bacon, she sighed as her phone resumed its incessant buzz-and-chime combo. She checked it to find the time was 9:30 a.m., and that she had a dozen missed calls and twenty-two text messages.

"Oh my God. Sheila's bridal shower!"

No time to finish, she stuffed her cheeks full of the mini-croissant and snatched a piece of bacon for the road. Before she raced out, she retrieved a shiny new penny from her purse. With a kiss to heads, she placed it next to the monitor on Alex's desk, heads side up.

As she rushed out the door, Madison couldn't help but notice the contents of his trash. The headline of the *Wall Street Journal* were the only words in English. *Is the rest in Chinese?*

Curiosity aside, she had things to do and places to be. Hurrying past Gina's office toward the elevator, she heard the suave voice call after her.

"This way's faster."

Trusting that her new friend, Mr. Robles, knew his way around much better than she did, she backtracked and followed him to a hidden second elevator.

"Your chariot awaits," he said, the car ready and waiting.

She stepped in, surprised as he joined her, pressing the button labeled *L*.

"Thank you. I'm terribly late," Madison said, prepared to explain how her best friend's bridal shower was happening and she was supposed to be picking up the cake, but she absentmindedly trailed off as her gaze landed on his ears.

His tanned earlobes were now sparkling, each adorned with two carats of shimmery elegance.

He raised an eyebrow, pulling his lips into an adorable smirk. "You said I could have them."

I did say that, didn't I?

They reached the lobby in seconds, and the elevator doors opened behind the security desk.

"I'll drive," Paco said, leading her to the executive garage.

Madison followed, in too much of a hurry to notice the luxuriousness of the car they'd gotten into. Her first clue was the telltale image of a charging bull on the steering wheel.

The strong growl of the Lamborghini seemed loud enough to wake the city, leaving Madison awestruck at the power reverberating clear through her seat. The second she clicked her seat belt in place, they raced onto the bustling streets of a Manhattan morning. Nervously, she clutched the door handle, and her observant driver slowed in response.

"Hey, you've got nothing to worry about. If you're in a car with me, consider yourself safe. Cars are my passion. I like my cars like I like my men—fast, powerful, and sexy when wet."

"Mr. Robles?" she asked.

"Please, call me Paco," he said, charming her with his smile.

"Paco, I'm sorry to ask, but do you mind if we drop by—"

"A bakery for Sheila's cake, and then to the restaurant for the bridal shower? I got you, girl. Cake's already been delivered, with flowers and a gift basket of Moët, gourmet chocolates, two Broadway tickets, and a card from you. We'll be at the restaurant in about fifteen minutes. You'll be right on time."

Blinking, Madison just stared at him.

He glanced at her. "Too much? I can keep the tickets if it would make you more comfortable," he said with a chuckle.

Nervously, she followed suit at his absurd display of selflessness. "I'm seriously afraid to ask how you know all that."

With a finger to his lips and a coy *shush*, he said, "I never reveal my sources." His smile grew wide. "Let me ask you something. Have you ever wondered what it would be like to have your every wish granted, and every desire anticipated? Well, Miss Madison, you're about to find out."

"I am?"

Dozens of questions whirled through her mind. But timing was everything, and Paco was pulling the car to the curb in front of the restaurant, where a gaggle of Madison's friends casually waited outside. Between her hot Latin driver and the sexy beast of a car, she instantly realized what this must look like.

Her friends' mouths dropped open as they stared. She smiled nervously, struggling to figure out how the hell to open the door. Suddenly, it opened for her.

Feeling sheepish, Madison stepped out, taking Paco's extended hand. He discreetly slipped an access card into it.

In a low voice, he said, "There's a message on your phone with my number. Text me when you're ready to leave."

Before any of her girlfriends could swarm him, he peeled away, the high-performance engine roaring down the city street.

Surrounding her instead, they tossed her question after question, giddy with enthusiasm at the man now labeled as her date.

"It's not like that. He's just a friend from work. Trust me, I'm *not* his type. And before you even ask, neither are any of you. Let's get set up."

As they headed into one of the private rooms, Madison found it filled with gorgeous rose-and-peony flower arrangements, a table ready for gifts, a champagne station, and dozens of appetizers. "Oh my gosh, I'm sorry I wasn't here to help. It looks amazing."

"Hellooo," one of her friends said. "We just walked in with you. We didn't do this."

Madison and the girls looked at each other blankly.

"Maybe we have the wrong room," Madison said slowly, wondering aloud.

But the congratulations, sheila sign on the table was flanked by the basket of goodies Paco promised.

Hiding her glee, she knew exactly who the culprit was behind this over-the-top display. Protectively, she went into stealth mode. And nothing helped a covert operation like a full-on booze distraction.

Armed with a glass of bubbly from the champagne station and a knife, she clinked the glass. "Well, someone put a whole lot of effort into what will be an amazing shower. And I for one am grateful."

The space filled with joyous laughter and the pops of champagne corks as the girls helped themselves to the glorious array of bubbly. When Sheila walked in a moment later, Madison handed her a glass.

"To the most gorgeous and amazing bride-to-be. To Sheila!" She held her glass high in the air, and the tinkle of glasses clinking sounded around the room.

With the food served, Madison enjoyed the never-ending feast, a few more glasses of champagne, and several rounds of avoiding questions about Paco or the party.

Bullet dodged.

Faint chimes and a string of buzzes pulsed from her phone. Downing the last of her glass of champagne, she checked her phone, seeing two text messages from different numbers.

UNKNOWN NUMBER, RECEIVED AN HOUR AGO: Text me back when you're ready to be picked up. PR

UNKNOWN NUMBER, RECEIVED 1 MINUTE AGO: Need you. Go to the room next door.

Forking a strawberry, Madison dredged it through the remaining buttercream frosting on her plate, savoring the very last bite of her second slice of cake.

"Be right back," she whispered to Sheila, then slipped away. But before she could knock on the door down the hall, the door swung open. "Alex!"

It was all she could say before he whisked her into the room and pulled her to the heat of his body. His eager kiss lingered as his tongue swept through her lips in long, languid strokes. He finally released her mouth and they both blew out satisfied breaths.

Leaning his forehead to hers, Alex said, "I missed you." He kissed her again, smoothing his hand over her cheek. "How's the party? Is everything acceptable?"

Scolding him playfully, she said, "I think you know *acceptable* isn't exactly the right term."

The muscles holding her against him tensed before he pulled back, and a furrow appeared across his brow.

Melting into a smile, Madison caressed his face, dropping her thumb to soothe the dimple in his chin. "No, it's not acceptable because it's remarkable. Beyond belief. But how did you know?"

She hoped her words came off as more curious than concerned and suspicious. But they were likely heavy with the weight of everything she wondered.

"When I moved your purse to the table, your phone slipped out. A text was on the screen confirming this morning's party of twenty at Le Reve's. I didn't want to wake you, but I didn't want something missed on account of me. So I called the restaurant and made sure you were taken care of." Boyish and sweet, Alex asked, "Is that, um, suitable?"

Madison kissed him, tightening her embrace and enjoying the

feel of the man in her arms. With his hot hands caressing her back, there was no room to keep up her guard.

Between them, it didn't feel like he was playing games. Even if he'd done nothing for her event, her reaction would have been the same. She didn't need any of it. Having Alex here was more than enough.

With a charming half smile, he asked, "So, I take it that's a yes?"

In response, she kissed him again, much slower this time. The warmth of his lips and the heat of his body melded with his scent, the scent that was distinctly Alex Drake. An intoxicating swirl that made her weak in the knees and wetter than a river in a rain forest.

It was all too much—his rugged good looks, tempting body, generosity, and kindness, all wrapped up in a scorching kiss and stone-hard bulge pressing into her like a battering ram. Madison wanted him more with every second that passed.

Again, they pulled away for a desperate breath. He was staring at her lips, and she licked them.

"What do you want?" she whispered.

"I'm dying for your mouth," he said, brushing his knuckles against her full bottom lip. His eyes met hers, patient as he waited.

"Yes," Madison said breathlessly, enjoying the feel of his fingers on her kiss-swollen lips.

Releasing her, he locked the door and led her to a wingback chair tucked in the corner of the room. Before he could undo his belt, she gripped his hands, placing them at his sides.

"It's your turn," she said, watching as his eyes darkened in approval.

Taking her time, she slipped off his slacks and boxers, letting them fall to his ankles. Then she sat him down, kneeling before him, reverent in worshipping his thick cock heavy in her hands.

He pulled her into a kiss, plunging his tongue through her lips, and priming her mouth for more.

She swiped her tongue wide across the fullness of his head, savoring the delicious drop at his tip that tasted a hundred times better than that bite of frosting had.

Alex's hands were on her, forcing her dress down to expose her breasts, aching for his touch with hard, puckered peaks. Gently, he cupped and caressed the soft, weighty mounds, increasing the pressure enough to make her body hum, and she moaned.

He plucked one before pressing it in his fingers. A soft squeal escaped her, and he repeated the teasing pinch with her other breast. Before losing much more control, she dropped her head, hungry for the rigid firmness of his shaft.

The second her mouth engulfed him, he sank back with a groan. His fingers wove into her hair, guiding her, and pushing her further with a deep growl.

"Yes," he insisted.

Having him like this, Madison moved with passion and longing, her body squirming with need. Her wetness seeped past her panties, her pussy ripe and ready, weeping for more.

She hollowed her cheeks, sucking hard and stroking his massive rod in tandem. He murmured her name, and she bobbed faster. But she had to see his face.

For a moment, she pulled away from his thick, silky shaft, letting her hands wrap him, balancing the clockwise and counter-clockwise strokes together. She worked them faster.

"God, Madison, you're going to make me come." His face was beautiful and relaxed.

Determined, she returned her mouth to him, sucking the living sin right out of that gorgeous cock. Without breaking her rhythm, she could feel him—dragging her skirt up, inching it across her back. His fingers swiped in circles across her ass and thighs. She squirmed, desperate to keep her steady pace.

His tender touch pushed her hips to a wanting rhythm, moving in unison with her head sliding up and down his length. Her back arched and her body moved, craving his penetrating touch.

His daring finger slid beneath her thong, grazing her between her cheeks before discovering her slick folds. He pressed a finger in, causing her to quiver and release a muffled squeal.

After a few pumps, he pulled her panties down, letting them fall to her knees. He smeared her wetness up and down her swollen pussy before plunging two fingers deep inside. Moaning around his shaft, she sped up as he fingered her—fucked her. His touch was so tender and yet so hard, she'd give anything to find her bliss in the sweet torture of his touch.

Faster, he pushed his pace, and her mouth raced to match his stride. They both groaned in pleasure. He would be hers. And unconditionally, she was his.

Her core quivered, tightening in a wave of pulses around his fingers. Slowing her breaths but maintaining her rhythm, she found holding out was becoming impossible.

When he pressed a third finger to her clit, the spasms rocked her, followed by a muffled succession of screams, and she forced him deep in her throat.

Out of control, her entire body shuddered, crashing her turbulent climax around his fingers and grinding them to a halt. But as he nudged her head just the slightest bit deeper, he exploded. She savored every last hot drop of him down her throat.

Drawing his fingers from the tightness of her core, he swept her onto his lap, cuddling her with soft kisses before sweeping his tongue in and tasting himself from her mouth.

Lazily, she watched as he sucked his fingers clean, lapping up every last drop of her sweetness. Madison was breathless as his gaze danced back at her.

His hand caressed her, moving down her body to the long line of her thigh. He snagged her panties, pulling them off her legs, and slipped them into his pocket.

After a few wonderful minutes resting in each other's arms, he stood, still cradling her tightly. Setting her in the chair, he replaced the dress back over her bodice, then whispered in her ear.

"I want you in my life, Madison. And not just for today."

Their kiss was slow. She clung to the ebbing seduction.

Breaking away, he rubbed his nose against hers, and his eyes twinkled as he smiled. "At whatever pace you're comfortable with."

Spent, she could only agree with a subtle nod.

Alex stood, straightening his shirt and blazer, then smoothed his hair from the steaming hot-sex god of a moment ago. Casually, he strolled behind her, warming her shoulders with his hands, and melting her with a quick massage. Her heavy eyes closed as she moaned.

"I have to go, beautiful. Rest, but not for too long. Your friends will wonder where you are."

He kissed her lightly on the head, then left.

MADISON DID her best to compose herself as she checked her hair and face in the reflection of her phone. Slipping out of the room and back into the bridal shower, she wondered if her escapade was obvious from her beaming smile or shaky walk.

As soon as she stepped in, Sheila shouted, "Maddi, I almost left. Where have you been?"

Breathing through the flush rising in her cheeks, she apologized. "Sorry, something came up." *Big-time.* "I was longer than I thought I'd be."

But only because he was longer than I thought he'd be.

CHAPTER 18

MADISON

Madison shot a text to Paco, and in an instant the rumble of the Lamborghini announced its presence from down the street. Somehow, the magnificent beast looked distinctly different.

As the scissor door lifted, she leaned down to ask, "Did your car change color, or was it red when you dropped me off?"

Laughing, Paco said, "I can't be seen wearing the same outfit twice." Gesturing to his suit, he emphasized that he'd also changed his outfit, though the flashes of brilliance remained on his dazzling ears.

Madison got in. "Okay, Mr. Mind Reader, where do I want to go now?" she asked, curious as to the extent of his precognition.

"Obviously, you *think* you want to go home. You've had a long day and you need to put your feet up, maybe lounge in a hot bath and get to bed early. Am I right?"

He is so right, it's scary. Like he's known me forever. Or maybe he just knows that any woman would want that after a long night followed by a long day.

She hid her giggle, wondering how many more times she could think of something *long*.

"But we're not doing any of that just yet," he said, handing her a small box.

"Oh, you shouldn't have."

Her excited statement ended on a down note when she opened the box. Madison lifted out the pair of used leather gloves, unsure what to think of them. They were fingerless, with a pattern of tiny holes punched across the top.

"I'll give you three chances," he said, inviting her to guess with a ridiculously adorable popped brow and thoroughly evil smile.

"Golfing?" Madison said, giving him a confused look.

"Nope."

"With this car and these gloves, we could be making a music video?"

"Good guess, with definite future potential, but not today."

Noticing their size, Madison slipped them on, which fit like, well, you know. Scrunching her brow, she thought aloud.

"Well, I can't be helping you bury a body." She wiggled her fingers. "Nothing's covering my fingerprints."

"So, you won't be my patsy? Noted. But I'm not giving you a hint."

"Oh, I don't need a hint. Obviously, you're letting me drive your car, and don't want my grubby hands mucking up your steering wheel." She smirked, knowing if she was going to bomb the last guess, she'd wrap it in a hopeful suggestion.

"Now who's the mind reader?" Paco said before taking a sudden turn onto an isolated road.

Madison held her breath. "Really? You're going to let me drive your car?"

"Look around," Paco said as he pointed out the lush density of vegetation surrounding them. "No, I'm going to have you help me bury a body."

The seriousness of his tone made her wonder for half a second, before she caught the tiniest hint of a smile.

The road opened to what seemed to be a secure area. no trespassing signs were posted along a border of twelve-foot-high double-chain-link fence topped with ropes of razor wire. The place had *we're not fucking around* written all over it.

The car rolled to a stop at an unmanned gate. A lone post held a small call box, a camera, and a swipe pad with DGI embossed on it.

Paco swiped his badge and the gate slid open. He revved the car forward, accelerating around several curves with a broad smile on his face. Once they drove through a mini forest, the tree cover ended to reveal a private runway with several hangars far ahead. At one end, he parked, opening both doors with the press of a button.

"Ready?" he asked.

No. Maybe.

"Yes," Madison said with a slight nod as she stepped out. Nervous, she headed to the driver's side as Paco stood waiting to help her in. "Wait. I don't think I can do this."

"Sure you can."

"I mean . . ." She blew out a long breath, hating to admit to a feminine shortcoming. "I don't know how to drive a standard."

"Yes, you and ninety-two percent of America. Lambos are all automatic. The highest performance automatic on the planet, in my opinion."

Automagically, Paco closed her winged door. Trying to hide her uncertainty, she bit her lip and hoped her arm didn't erupt in her usual wave of itchy patches.

As Paco slid beside her in the passenger seat, that door closed as well. Step by step, he ran through a crash course on the mechanics of the display and functions.

"This is a massive piece of machinery. Are you sure you want me driving it?"

Seriously, he leaned in, and she gave him her undivided attention.

"Miss Madison, before you start driving, there are three

things I need you to understand. One, you can't hurt anyone or anything. Look around," he said, and she did. "We're on a private runway in the middle of fucking nowhere. And you couldn't flip this baby if you tried. Okay?"

"Yes, okay." Madison deliberately relaxed her shoulders with a sigh of relief.

"Good. Two, I'm not just going to let you drive so you get a quick high like we're a couple of kids at an amusement park. I want to teach you a few tricks with this car, share with you some really cool shit, but I can only do that if you listen to me very carefully and trust me without question. Got it?"

"Got it." Feeling more confident, Madison nodded. "And three?"

"Three, the gloves you're wearing aren't just to keep your grubby little hands from mucking up my steering wheel. That's only half the reason."

Madison exaggerated her eye roll.

Gently, Paco lifted her hand and continued. "Those gloves were previously owned by the remarkable Cha Cha Muldowney, also known as the First Lady of Drag Racing. She'd go from a dead stop to two hundred twenty-six feet in five and a half seconds. She'd break two hundred sixty miles per hour in a hot pink car, kicking ass and looking damn good doing it. She was brave in the face of adversity, and fierce to those who dared to challenge her. Channel her spirit and glamour at all times when you drive this car. I certainly do. Clear?"

"Yes," Madison said with sass, trying on Paco's badass vibe for size.

As he nudged her with a sexy smile and waggling brow, Madison started the engine. Her body jolted, startled at the strong growl emanating from the car and vibrating her ass. Loudly, she giggled.

Taking command and easing her breaths, she looked over at Paco, inspired by his insistent nod communicating, *Get it, girl!*

Slamming her foot on the gas, she peeled off, squealing with delight as the car hit ninety miles per hour in seconds.

Although she couldn't hear him, Paco windmilled his arm in the air, shouting over and over what looked like, "More! More!"

Madison hit 120 miles per hour before slowing, flipping a U-turn, and gunning it even harder. Her smile stretched from ear to ear. At the end of the runway, breathless with exhilaration, she slowed as Paco motioned for her to come to a stop.

He gave her a huge grin. "Having fun?"

Too winded for words, she nodded.

"Ever heard of a J-turn?"

"No, but I'm familiar with a three-point turn. Is it like that?"

"Yes," Paco said excitedly. "Think of it as a three-point turn without the middle point. We're going to start in reverse. When you get to about thirty-five miles per hour, you're going to whip the steering wheel like this without letting up on the gas. This will lock the front wheels. Then yank the steering wheel hard in the exact opposite direction. As soon as the front of the car has slid a hundred eighty degrees from the direction you were in, pop it into drive and gun it. Got it?"

Blankly, she blinked. Catching on to the sheer depths of his lunacy, she blurted, "No! I got none of that. At all. I have no idea what you just said."

"Cool, then this will be way more fun than I thought. Oh, and if we really want some fun . . ." He opened the glove compartment and pulled out a satin blindfold. "One of us can wear this. Hmm, who should it be?"

Pointing back and forth between them and silently mouthing *eenie meenie miney mo,* he began sliding it over his head. With a nervous yelp, Madison yanked his arm down.

"Oh, you want it. Okay!" Paco leaned over with a playful growl as she resisted. Sternly, he reminded her of his words. "You said you'd trust me implicitly. Crazy trust test time. Put it on."

Reluctantly, Madison took the blindfold and put it on. After a few seconds, she opened her eyes from behind it.

"Hey," she said, shocked by the discovery. "I can see through this. Or have you somehow bestowed me with the power of X-ray vision?"

"Yes, you can see through it. So begins your afternoon of lessons. Lesson one. Things aren't always what they seem, or nearly as scary as they appear. Okay, lesson's over. Give that baby back. I'm going to need it for a little fun time later."

As he tossed the blindfold back into the glove box, Madison caught sight of more of his little props. *Did I just see fuzzy handcuffs? Not judging, and definitely not asking.*

Paco drew her attention. "So, let's go over this one more time, and then give it a try. In reverse, start driving, and when you get to thirty-five miles per hour, grab the steering wheel like so. Yank hard, then yank in the opposite direction. Once you complete the turn, lock the wheels, shift into drive, then accelerate to the end of the runway. Ready?"

"As ready as I'm gonna be."

Madison put the monstrous beast in reverse and pressed timidly on the gas. At the pivotal speed, she started yanking the steering wheel, but Paco pulled it much more forcefully.

The car began to spin. She yanked the wheel in the opposite direction just as forcefully, locking the wheels without needing Paco's assistance.

"Good," he said, and returned his hand to his lap.

With the car now facing the opposite direction, she popped it into drive, slammed her foot to the gas, and floored it, propelling the precision machine to 135 miles per hour before easing it to a stop.

Proud as a badass peacock, she beamed. Her heart pounded out of her chest, and her head spun, making her dizzy with excitement. "Oh my God, that was incredible!"

"You did pretty good. Ready to try again on your own?"

"Yes!" she exclaimed, then caught the *on your own* part. Feigning confidence, she sucked in a breath.

Paco pointed ahead. "Good. Pull up there, let me out, and let's see what you've got."

She nodded, grinning with the giddiness of a girl who was bypassing the line and getting to ride the awesome roller coaster again. When she pulled up to the vacant area he instructed, he got out.

Paco leaned in, giving her a few more instructions. "Do it twice. Once going down there to the end, then once again on your way back. Go really freaking fast and hurry up. If I break a sweat out here, I'll be super cranky." He stepped away, and the door shut.

Madison got the car into position, and slowly rolled in reverse.

Bond. Madison Bond.

After testing the waters with a bit more gas, she pressed her foot hard, going for broke. With Paco watching, the Lamborghini moved with surprising ease as she executed the maneuver twice, once down, and a second later, once back.

With all the thrill and speed of a Formula Rossa roller coaster, the buildup climbed to the point of full throttle, and in seconds was sadly over. Still giddy in the aftermath, she returned to pick up Paco.

Although she pulled up right next to him, his utter annoyance was apparent. Arms crossed and head shaking, he stalked to the driver's side. As the door winged up, he tapped his foot in irritation.

Dramatically, he slid his sunglasses down his nose to glare at her. "You may have kicked ass with that last J-turn, but this ain't your car, Miss M."

Dropping his vexed facade and exchanging it for a wide grin, he offered his hand to help her out, which she quickly accepted. Keeping her composure was impossible. Once her feet touched the ground, she bounced gleefully, shouting a *hell yeah* as she bopped over to the passenger side.

As he drove off the runway and out of the foreboding entry point, Paco resumed his lesson. "And that leads us to lesson two. You're capable of more than you think. There are great things in store for you, Miss Madison. Trust your instincts. Always."

Awestruck, she stared. "So, do you prefer Yoda or Sensei? Um, I don't mean to sound ungrateful, because this was utterly amazing, but why did you teach me all this?"

For the first time since she'd met him, Paco looked somber, the shine draining from his eyes.

"What's wrong?" Madison asked. "Was it something I said?"

"Oh, it's just my RBF," he said, forcing a smile.

"You have a resting bitch face like I have a third boob. What is it?"

CHAPTER 19

PACO

Paco looked over, melting at the familiar warmth in Madison's eyes.

He got it—why Alex had been drawn in so quickly. It was as clear as the perfect button nose on her face. Her eyes and her smile, whipped together in a perfect recipe of sincerity and understanding, made keeping his guard up around her impossible.

But he needed to pull it together. For all their sakes.

"Let's just say I really wanted to teach this to someone once. Someone very special. But I lost the chance." He took a needed breath. Looking at her, he shared a harmless bit of honesty, even if its full meaning would be lost on her. "I guess I just didn't want to miss the chance again."

Still in her seat belt, Madison leaned over and rested her head on his shoulder in a silent display of empathy.

Paco's heart sank. Sometimes, there are no words for loss. Just understanding. In that, he and Madison would be forever connected.

His glassy eyes remained focused on the road, but he rested

his head on hers as they quietly made their way back into the city.

～

PACO DROVE AROUND THE CORNER, heading toward Madison's apartment. The street was a hellacious labyrinth of double-parked cars and crowds of overzealous pedestrians. He looked up, quickly finding her humble abode crammed amongst the squeeze of windows climbing six stories high.

Teasing her, he slowed, then sped past without a glance. When she gave him a worried frown and a soft touch on his forearm, he broke out in a practiced maniacal laugh.

"Don't bother asking. We're doing exactly what I said you would do. Promise."

"Really? Because I believe you distinctly said something about lounging in a bath and an early bedtime." After a second of Paco continuing to keep her in suspense, she asked, "Can you at least give me a hint?"

"There's something you need to learn about this inner circle. We're vaults. Bat those big pretty eyes all you want, but there will be absolutely, positively no hints."

The irritation pouring from her scrunched-up face and pouty lip was too adorable for words. And he didn't need to snap a shot with his phone to remember. Every face he'd ever seen would be permanently filed away for safekeeping.

And today, the many looks of Madison Taylor would forever be locked away in a very special corner of the vast vault of his mind.

CHAPTER 20

MADISON

Madison admired her new friend's handsome face long after he'd turned his attention to the road. His instructions were clear and wrapped around her like a warm blanket. Trust your instincts.

I trust you, Paco Robles.

With a few quick turns, they were nearing the DGI skyscraper as he asked, "Do you have that card I gave you?"

Carefully opening her elegant Hermès clutch, Madison pulled out the little card he'd handed her earlier, waving it with a smile.

"Good, you'll need it."

"I will?" she asked, realizing they were now passing DGI's headquarters.

"Yes," he said before she could ask the question. "We're going the wrong way for that too." Her amused glare made him chuckle. "And that's all you're getting out of me for now."

Between the warm sunshine beaming through the windshield, the purr of the engine lulling her in the leather seat, and the closeness she felt with her new friend, Madison couldn't stifle the yawn that crept up on her. She wrestled with a few heavy blinks before sinking back and swearing to close her eyes for just a moment.

~

MADISON WOKE to Paco killing the engine. Shaking off her disorientation, she took a curious glance around. They were in a very private, very upscale garage with custom lighting and a glossy finish to the designer floors.

Her door opened with Paco standing outside. "We're here." Again, he offered a hand to help her out, which she accepted with a gracious smile.

"Where?" Madison asked, not recognizing it.

"Where you'll be staying . . . unless you object. I confess, my driving lesson was to keep you occupied until Alex finished this up for you. Use your card over there."

Madison headed to an elevator, ready to give the panel a swipe with the card she held. In an instant, Paco's hand covered hers, stopping her before she could complete the move.

A solemn expression overtook his face, though his smile remained intact. "You have my number. If you need to leave for any reason, text me. No questions asked."

Curious, she gripped his hand in both of hers. "You're concerned?"

Insistently, he shook his head. "No. Not about leaving you here. But I know how fast this is all happening for you. Each step is a decision. Maybe a hard one. Maybe one you shouldn't have to make right away. I don't want you worrying about having second thoughts. You're entitled to them. If an hour from now or a week from now, you want your space, I'll be your chariot and will happily lead-foot you anywhere you want to go."

Madison took a breath, thinking through his sweet offer. There was a kinship between them. This polished man in his pristine suit and Italian shoes cared for her with a warmth that she couldn't put her finger on, like a best friend she'd known for years. Almost like family.

"Look," she said, leading with complete candor. "You and I don't know each other. But I feel like we do."

He nodded with a grin. "I feel the same way," he said with a humble tone that seemed uncommon and special.

"Which means I know I can level with you on this. And that somehow, you'll understand. This connection I feel with Alex, it's like the one I feel with you."

Playfully, Paco lifted a brow. "Not exactly."

Madison giggled. "No, not exactly. But it's there. It's tangible. I sense it with everything I am, and I can't explain it, but I feel like I don't need to." She took a solemn breath. "Have I mentioned my brother, Jack?"

Serious and reserved, Paco shook his head.

"We lost Jack, and I think of him a lot. Did he do everything he wanted his last day? What if it's my last day?"

"It's not." Paco's voice was defiant and stern, his hard expression revealing his panic.

Calmly, she shushed him with a grin. "All I mean is if it were, maybe I'd forgo the run and have a second slice of bridal shower cake. Maybe I'd get behind the wheel of a car worth more than my apartment building and floor the gas pedal. And maybe, just maybe, I'd take a chance on the sweet man at the office who goes out of his way to get me my favorite drink when he should be more concerned with running his global empire. See? Easy decision."

Paco pulled her in for a warm hug. "Yes, Miss Madison. Easy decision."

They both pulled in a deep breath as they leaned into each other. Even though she was sure Paco sniffled, Madison said nothing, focused on controlling her pesky tears.

Finally, he released her. "Well, what are you waiting for? That key card isn't going to swipe itself."

Giddy with the growing butterflies tickling her insides, she swiped. The doors slid open, revealing a similar panel inside the elevator. Nodding as he stepped in beside her, Paco encouraged her to swipe again, so she did. With no buttons to push, the doors closed and the car lifted them quickly.

When the doors reopened, Madison stood there, overwhelmed at the sight of the luxury penthouse apartment overlooking the city. Pale blush roses were set in vases throughout a room of expensive furnishings, exquisite paintings, and bronze figurines that looked antique. The wall of windows showcased a view of Manhattan's skyline that was breathtaking.

Stunned, Madison froze to stare, so Paco gently led her in. His hand lightly pressed the small of her back as she stammered out, "W-wha—"

"Welcome home, Miss Madison. Enjoy discovering. Dinner will be served at seven o'clock. Your bath is already drawn and will hold its temperature for about an hour. And it bears repeating—call or text me if you need anything. At all."

With a quick kiss on each of her cheeks, he stepped back into the elevator.

Still at a loss for words, Madison could only question him with her wide eyes.

Brushing aside her unasked question with nothing more than a grin, he said, "And don't lose those gloves. You'll need them again." He winked at her just before the elevator doors shut.

Did he say home?

THE VASTNESS of the penthouse apartment was remarkable, but that paled in comparison to its contents. The furnishings and art were exquisite, yet warm and cozy. Books were abundant in each room, some new and some old, and many with bookmarks, as if they'd been re-shelved mid-read.

Meandering through the halls, she stepped shyly into the master bedroom. The breathtaking space was flooded with light from the floor-to-ceiling windows as well as four oversized skylights. Wonder and a tingling blush filled her as she stared for a minute at the oversized bed.

Wait. What kind of billionaire lets a strange woman loose in his place? I could be a crazy woman. Rifling through his stuff. Stealing his shit. Jumping on his bed. With. My. Shoes. On.

And if Madison was in for a penny, she was hell-to-the-yeah in for a pound. Tiptoeing, she stepped into what she presumed was Alex's closet. But she was very, very wrong.

Oh my God. The semi-palace held a wide range of elegant women's clothing, tags intact. Frantically, she flipped through a dozen or so in disbelief. They were all in her size.

It was as if Rodeo Drive had backed up a truck and unloaded its load of high-end clothes and accessories right into the elegant room. A wall of shelves held an unbelievable variety of shoes for every season, arranged by color and heel height, and again, all in her size. But it didn't hold every pair.

Inside a special alcove, a pedestal sat below a spotlight, showcasing the pair Alex had given her. Smiling and sentimental, she brushed them softly with her fingertips. Glancing around, she still couldn't believe her eyes.

I can practically do a J-turn right here in this space. This closet is nearly the size of my apartment.

The center of the closet was taken up by an island with a much smaller version of the DGI access panel. When she hovered her card across it, it opened, a reverse Venus flytrap exposing boxes from Tiffany's and Cartier.

Looking down at her wrist, she decided the diamonds wrapping it were plenty. She swiped the panel again and the island closed, keeping all its wonders safe and sound.

Curious, Madison followed the sound of a slight rumbling from the other end of the closet. She emerged into a bathroom with a huge white bathtub front and center, surrounded by water flowing from its infinity edging.

The rumbling was from a series of Jacuzzi jets, pulsing lavender-scented water in an intoxicating swirl that she had to touch. It felt like heaven.

A side panel displayed the temperature, with the ability to adjust it up and down. *I am not messing with perfection.* Next to the temperature panel was a plush robe with *MT* embossed on the pocket.

She looked around. Half the towels were embossed with her initials, and the other half labeled *AD* in identical stitching.

Next to the bathtub, a bottle of champagne was chilling in a bucket of ice beside a single flute. A small table next to it held a tray of chocolate-covered strawberries, cheeses, and artisan crackers. A little note with madison handwritten on it was tucked on the tray, and she opened it.

Enjoy your bath. See you tonight.
Alex

Seeing his name made her smile.

The note? The bath? And the outrageously gorgeous apartment?

What's a girl to do?

Perhaps this wasn't *home* in all that the word entailed. But for the moment, it was wondrous and warm, and made her feel more comfortable than she'd ever felt before. And it wasn't about the things. It was all Alex. He was sweet and thoughtful, and went so far out of his way to make her welcome, she couldn't help but feel close to him.

Madison knew, more than most, that life was short. It all begged to be savored. And savor it, she sure as hell would.

CHAPTER 21

MADISON

After indulging in a bath, sipping champagne, tasting some delectable strawberries, and slipping on a little black dress that flawlessly walked the fine line between elegant and casual, Madison was ready to see Alex.

There was still time before dinner, and she wasn't exactly sure when he'd be there. *Home*, she reminded herself.

To fill the time, she lost herself in the penthouse the way one loses their day in a fine museum. The furnishings and art were stunning yet subdued, and in a strange way, exactly to her liking. Each item was something she would have chosen. You know, if she had unlimited resources and a penchant for really expensive stuff.

She admired how every piece seemed to be placed in the exact spot she would have put them. Even the book on the side table, lying perfectly off-center beneath the lamp.

The Count of Monte Cristo. Her favorite.

She picked it up, thumbing through it nostalgically. Heaving a sigh, she finally flipped back to the very first page, and her smile vanished. The beautiful inscription there was handwritten in cursive.

Love you always.
Grandpa Mike

Reeling in shock, she closed the book and carefully inspected the cover and spine before reopening it. Stunned, she stared in disbelief.

This is my book. From Grandpa Mike. A book that up until that day had been in her apartment, tucked away in a drawer next to her bed.

Alarmed and clutching the thick vintage book, she scanned the room, wondering exactly what she'd walked into. In one corner of the room was a sleek black baby grand piano, its top adorned with about a dozen framed photos.

A fairly small one caught her eye. In it, she and her father seemed to be posing, and holding up another photo. Squinting and frustrated, she couldn't make out the photo-within-the-photo, but three people were in the smaller image.

It's too fuzzy. I can't tell who they are. But that's my dad, and that's definitely me at fourteen or maybe fifteen.

Undeniably, the two of them were smiling, posing for the shot. She had only the faintest recollection of the photo being taken, and none of whatever it was they were holding. The more she tried recalling it, the more of a blank slate her mind became.

Her head was swimming with emotions and questions. Mostly questions.

Despite her initial thoughts, *how* might not be the biggest question. She got it. Alex was a billionaire whose company specialized in reconnaissance and surveillance, data mining, and, of course, investigating. He certainly had the resources.

No, the biggest question was *why*.

Retracing her steps back to her purse, she pulled out her phone and snapped a shot of the interior of the book, then the photo.

She sent the images to the number Alex had texted from earlier, making her point with only three capital letters.

MADISON: WTF?!

CHAPTER 22

PACO

At 6:30 p.m. sharp, Paco picked up Alex from his last meeting of the day in the Lamborghini, a common practice they both found helpful. The drive allowed them to catch up on any recent developments at work, and on whatever else was on their minds, with a casual familiarity they both preferred not to reveal at the office.

To the outside world, Paco and Alex were merely employer and employee. Only they knew the depth of their friendship.

Even with the long hours, nothing beat carrying on with work in a half-million-dollar car. Paco could get places quickly, and pretty much park wherever the hell he wanted.

He alone was trusted with highly confidential transactions, covert reconnaissance, and anything that required just the right touch when hundreds of millions of dollars were on the line.

Today, a few documents required Alex's signature. The slightest premature leak of the information contained within them could impact DGI in a very long-term and detrimental way.

And what these documents contained, if taken out of context, could incite semi-mass hysteria. Crash global markets. Kill their stock value overnight. Place DGI in the international hot seat for years to come.

But this was Alex, and how he rolled. *Just another day.*

Conversely, if tidbits of information needed to hit the streets, Alex had the connections and Paco had the network. They scattered leaks strategically, planting each in an optimal climate with pinpoint precision. DGI's stock value, corporate growth, and global presence were solidified.

And with each notch on the DGI bedpost of lucrative transactions, an equally impressive bonus always followed, flowing straight to Paco's offshore bank account.

A speed reader, Alex breezed through the documents, signing here and initialing there, easily multitasking when a text alert diverted his attention. With a quick glance, he read his phone while signing, and his signature stuttered, scrawling clear off the page.

"Fuck," he muttered under his breath.

Paco, witnessing Alex's faux pas, dismissed his concern. "Don't worry. I have a second set for just these times when you stroke out during an important signature." Helpfully, he reached over to point out the binder's second tab.

"No, *this!*"

Scouting about for a place to park, Paco pulled into the nearest valet drop-off point, in front of a restaurant. As the valet scurried to let him out and take the keys, Paco lowered the power window.

"Hey, I just need to sit here for a minute," he said, handing the man a hundred-dollar bill. Raising the window, he ignored the gush of gratitude and focused on the text Alex just received. He pulled it closer, getting a better look at the images.

Letting out a long breath, Paco handed back the phone. "Are you going to tell her?"

Pensively, Alex stared off in the distance. "Not yet."

Paco unleashed a controlled amount of irritation. "Why not? You said yourself you didn't want to hide everything at your place, or start a relationship on the wrong foot. So, here you are. At this point, I'm not sure you can avoid it."

Alex just maintained his faraway stare, seeming to contemplate the damn good advice. After a minute or two of silence, he made his decision.

"What I can't avoid . . . I might be able to delay." Alex's statement came off as a question, with a distinct tone of requesting Paco's advice.

Paco looked away, making up his own mind without being pressured by the weight of their past. He knew the importance of the unasked question. With an unsure shrug, he finally conceded with a nod.

"Let's go," Alex said as he sent a text, most likely to Madison.

With that, Paco peeled away from the restaurant.

CHAPTER 23

MADISON

Deep in thought, Madison sat gazing out the window, staring unseeing at the Manhattan skyline. *I need answers.* But deep down, she wavered, hating confrontation.

The waiting was making her nervous and edgy. There was no stopping the hive rash from breaking out on her arm. She stifled an itch and rested her head back against the chair as she waited.

For the eighth or ninth time in a row, she read Alex's text.

> ALEX: *Please don't go. I'll be there in fifteen minutes. Maybe faster. Paco's driving.*

Rattled and still unsure how to even handle this bizarre situation, she sucked in a breath as the bell rang.

He's ringing the bell?

Getting her bearings, she headed toward the elevator as another set of soft pings hit the air. *How do I answer it?*

Without her intervention, the elevator opened. The soft murmur of unfamiliar voices broke the silence. Several people entered pushing stainless-steel rolling carts, halting as soon as they saw her.

A tall man wearing a catering apron addressed her. "Good evening, ma'am. We have instructions to set up in the small library, unless you prefer a different location?"

Not sure of what to say or do, she just nodded. "Sure. Thank you."

She followed them as they seemed to know their way around, setting up at a table with two chairs in a day room off to the side.

Feverishly, they worked to get a four-course meal set up at the table overlooking the city. As their arranging was coming to a close, Madison panicked, ready to scramble for her purse and give them a tip. But the moment they'd finished, they departed like food ninjas in the night.

Delectable wafts of food emanated from the elegant dinner setting. Several assorted plates were covered with silver domes, hiding the food beneath. Moët chilled in a polished stand, and a low arrangement of pale pink roses decorated the center of the table.

Before she could step forward and peek at the dishes emanating savory scents, the elevator pinged again.

She stepped out, frozen in place as Alex entered the apartment. He looked every bit the total package. A sweep-you-off-your-feet kind of guy with rugged good looks and a touch that absolutely undid her.

But was this all just the pretty wrapping to something much darker?

Everyone has a past. Could his be worse? Is he a stalker? How did he get the book and the photo? And what about the nickname he knew? Or my name, for that matter?

Alex's eyes, tortured and desperate, locked with hers, but he didn't move. Madison's heart raced out of her chest as their lovers' standoff played out.

CHAPTER 24

Alex kept Paco waiting in the car for a few reasons. He might need a wingman. Or a witness . . . in case he needed something signed. Or, God forbid, if Madison needed a ride.

But as he stood, not budging from the entrance to his penthouse suite, his gaze remained fixed on hers. Alex focused to keep his breathing steady. Controlled.

God, not now.

Desperate to suppress the growing pounding in his ears, he pushed aside his panic as he stared deep into her gorgeous, worried eyes. He needed to quiet his thoughts, push away the darkness and pain, and focus on nothing but her.

An episode, even a small one, would take center stage at the worst possible time. Madison couldn't find out about his weakness like this.

I have to be here for her. Protect her.

Alex could see as plain as day she was suppressing her own reactions. *Justified reactions.*

Sure, he'd seen her lash out once, but none of that was her nature. She'd snapped at Gina because she'd been pushed and provoked, and mostly because of him. And even then, Madison's first instinct was to leave.

She had to be considering it. Bolting as fast as possible away from this asylum and its inmate.

Please don't go.

Mindful, his gaze fell from her doleful expression to her hand on her arm. Instantly, her scratching stopped. *Her hives are back.* Despite the obvious itch driving up her skin, she was staying.

Relieved, he stepped closer.

"Alex, I'm not sure what's going on, and I'm not sure how long I can downplay the full extent of my total freak-out, but I'd really like to hear whatever it is you want to tell me. To understand it. All of it. How did you know my name? And about Igz? And how did you get my book? And the photo? Did you . . . did you break into my apartment?"

"No, on my life, I didn't." He had to embrace her, reassure her, but the doubt in her eyes stopped his advance cold. "I can only imagine what you're thinking. The answer is no, I didn't take your things."

"Then *how?*" Madison's expression demanded answers, her eyes searching his desperately.

Uneasy, Alex began to pace. *How do I tell her? And still keep my word?*

The terms were unwritten—barely a contract, if you asked Paco. But to Alex, it was a contract, a verbal agreement he would keep . . . no matter what anyone else thought.

Again, he took a step toward Madison, covering her shoulders with his hands and gently coaxing her to sit in a chair. He took a knee before her, grasping her hand with a tender caress.

Thinking fast, he had an idea. "Look, will you stay here for five minutes? Just don't leave. I'll be right back."

Madison studied his eyes, and patiently, he awaited her decision. He pled with his eyes, and when she finally nodded, he jumped to his feet.

Leaving the room, he made a quick call. "Meet me in my study."

In the room he used as his home office, Alex typed a quick letter and hit print, ready to give Madison Taylor an offer she couldn't refuse.

"You rang?" Paco asked, sarcastic as he entered, obviously leery of the scheme before Alex even uttered a word.

Flatly, Alex had to say it. "I could really use your support."

"How about we start with my skepticism and see where it goes?"

Determined, Alex whipped the fresh printout to his desk, penned his name, then handed it to Paco. "Sign this."

Paco took half a second to scan the single-page document. Looking back at Alex with a heated glare and pursed lips, he tossed it back onto the desk. "Nope."

"Sign it!"

"Have you lost your fucking mind?" Paco shouted.

Concerned, Alex shushed him, motioning toward the open door with a reminder of Madison not too far down the hall.

"Come on. Just sign it."

"Not happening. Go ahead—cancel my black card. Get someone else. I'm not signing it."

Cautiously, Alex proceeded. Paco's flight mode could flip to fight mode at a moment's notice.

Defenseless and showing it, Alex stood open armed and pleading with all he had. He didn't want a fight. But he stayed behind his desk, not wanting to get his ass kicked either, in case Paco was ready to pound some sense into him.

With a heavy breath, Alex considered his words and actions carefully. Then he said the one word he rarely said to the man, hoping with all his might it had some meaning between friends.

Softly, he said, "Please."

Paco began rambling, something he only did when he was

that perfect storm of freaked-the-fuck-out and completely comfortable letting it all go.

"Everything about this screams *bad idea.* You barely know her. *We* barely know her. Do I have to go down the full spectrum of possible ramifications? One wrong move and DGI could be cut off at the knees, practically dissolving everything we've all worked so hard for over the last decade. If I sign this, DGI might die a very quick death. You can't take this back, Alex."

Quietly, Alex calmed his emotions. "I've never asked you for anything."

"I know that!" Paco revealed his anger in a wild flailing of his arms, but refrained from shouting. "Goddammit, you think I don't know that?"

"I have to do this. Show her what's in my heart."

"Yeah? Didn't anyone ever tell you that the heart is the fucking Achilles heel of business? I'm here to protect you. You might be the majority shareholder of DGI, but I'm fucking second in line. If I do this, I might be failing you more than I ever have."

The somber meaning of his words hung heavy between them.

Direct and confident, Alex softly said, "It's her."

Paco's squint and pursed lips meant only one thing, and Alex smiled.

"Give me a goddamn pen before I change my mind." Signing, Paco said, "I always knew we'd go down in a ball of flames. I just never imagined I'd hand you the kerosene."

"Look, if we're going down like the Titanic, your ass is on a lifeboat. I'll take the hit alone."

"Let's get one thing straight. We go down together . . ." Paco's somber tone belied his knowing brow and cocky grin. "Or not at all."

Smiling with gratitude and patting Paco's shoulder, Alex said, "Do me another favor. Don't start blinging out your life preserver just yet."

CHAPTER 25

MADISON

Five minutes earlier

Madison watched as Paco stepped off the elevator. Before heading to meet Alex in his study, he paused to give her an assured smile and lifted a single finger, requesting her patience for a minute.

She didn't know exactly why, but seeing Paco was a relief. Not enough of one to stop the incessant itching on her arm, but it made her feel better anyway.

Waiting was torture, giving her mind time to come up with a million questions. At the top of the list were, *What's Alex doing? And why does he need Paco?*

Still, Madison wasn't exactly making a break for the door. Alex had her book and her photo. A photo of her teenage self might have been creepy, but her dad was in the shot.

She thought for a moment. When was the first time she and Alex met? Could it have been a long time ago, with her dad?

Madison needed answers, and so she'd wait it out, come hell or high water. At least, she thought that until Paco began shouting. His words came through loud and clear.

"Have you lost your fucking mind?"

Did Paco just discover something? About Alex?

The remainder of his words were muffled, but his tone was insistent, the sound of someone thoroughly pissed off.

It should have been her tipping point—enough for her to scurry away and never look back. But she had to stay. To get to the bottom of it.

As both men returned, Alex handed her the printed document with fresh signatures.

Madison read it, forcing herself to breathe. Done, she shot a look of disbelief to Alex, then Paco. Perplexed, she looked back to Alex.

Finally, she had the presence of mind to speak. "I'm not sure what to say, but I guess I'm with Paco. Because I'm pretty sure you've lost your fucking mind."

CHAPTER 26

MADISON

The letter bearing today's date read as follows:

To Whom It May Concern,

I, Alex Drake, being of sound mind, do hereby agree that if I ever lie to Madison Taylor, everything I have and everything I own, including my personal and corporate holdings, will immediately and unequivocally be transferred to her for whatever purpose she deems fit.

Signed,

Alex Drake
President and CEO
Drake Global Industries

Witnessed:
Paco Robles

Madison bounced a concerned glance between the two men,

then landed her glare on Paco, pouring every bit of *you've got to be kidding* straight at him. He shrugged, raising a *talk to the hand* palm to her face, his expression clearly expressing *don't even start.*

Alex returned to his bended-knee position before her, taking her free hand in both of his. "Madison, I promise you that the book and photo, as strange as it may sound, were given to me. I didn't take them . . . *or* have someone take them for me."

They both glanced at Paco.

"Why are you both looking at me?" Paco puffed up, seeming indignant at the implication. "Hey, these pristinely manicured nails are waaaay above petty theft."

Madison studied Alex's eyes, more confused than ever.

"The bottom line, Madison, is that I can't tell you, at this moment, why I know the things I know or have the things I have, but I promise you it's not what you're thinking . . . whatever you're thinking." Alex caressed her face in his hands, pulling her forehead to his. "I swear, every single thing is on the up-and-up. I just need a little time before I explain . . . and I *will* tell you everything. Please, will you stay?"

Between the warmth of his hands and the desperation in his eyes, Madison contemplated Alex's request for all of thirty seconds. *Yes.* Surprising even herself, her acceptance came out as another question.

"How much time?" she asked cautiously.

"Thirty days. And I'll tell you absolutely everything. All of it."

"Thirty days?" she said, considering his request.

If there was one thing Madison knew, it was people. After years in the service industry, she practically had a sixth sense for knowing who to trust and who to back away from. Her track record was solid.

Beyond a shadow of a doubt and for no reason at all, she trusted Alex Drake. A man she barely knew. But one who apparently trusted her with his home, and possibly the future of his company.

This is crazy.

With a deep breath and a silent prayer, she decidedly threw caution—and maybe common sense—to the wind.

"Okay. Thirty days," she said, acquiescing with a wave of raw emotions as his lips landed on hers in an impassioned kiss.

Interrupting, Paco cleared his throat. "Look, you both seem to have this sorted, so I'm just going to head out." He made a casual stroll to the elevator as Alex called after him.

"Hey," Alex said.

Paco turned back as the doors opened.

"Thank you. And if I didn't mention it earlier, nice earrings."

Grinning, Paco entered the elevator, letting the doors slide shut as he tossed back his defense. "She said I could have them."

CHAPTER 27

MADISON

Grateful at seeing Madison satisfied, at least for the moment, Alex couldn't avoid the direction of his relief. He was charged and more than ready to take her in his arms and never look back. Not like the others.

With any other woman, sex was just a trade-off. He got the no-strings-attached hookups his overactive libido needed, and they got what they wanted. Usually jewelry. Sometimes cash. The occasional gift of a flashy car ended a few of his booty calls.

But there was never intimacy, because Alex could never be intimate without trust. At least never again, a decision he'd made a very long time ago.

No one's getting close.

But Madison was different. He felt it in every fiber of his being and clear to the depths of his soul.

Look at her.

Even with a closet filled to the rafters with high-end jewels, the only piece on her was the extravagant tennis bracelet, and only because Paco had wrapped it around her wrist.

Madison was everything. Brave and honest, regardless of the consequences. Kind. Generous. She endeared herself to him even more, seeming practically oblivious to the fact she had all the makings of the girl next door wrapped up in the appearance of a fucking *Sports Illustrated* model.

She was perfect. In every single way.

Laying one passionate kiss on her lips after another, Alex was so damn grateful that she returned them willingly. Freely. Even passionately and enthusiastically.

His arms embraced her, pulling her tightly against him. Every soft curve of her body begged to be discovered. But a hot meal waited in the next room.

"You hungry?" he asked, stroking her cheek softly with his knuckles.

Madison remained quiet, not saying a word as she shook her head. Her slight smile widened, and the fullness of her lips invited his return. With each of her deep breaths, the rise and fall of her chest was subtle. Seductive. Whatever questions or doubts that remained between them seemed to fade away, leaving room for his lust and her surrender.

She was his.

And he wanted nothing more than to be hers.

Lifting her from the chair, he stood, cradling her in his arms. Making his way to the master bedroom, he was glad she'd be the very first to ever share his bed.

He set her on her knees on the large mattress, skimming a finger down her spine. His tongue pressed through her lips, parting them to explore, tasting her with deep, sweeping strokes.

He stripped off his pants as she tugged free his tie. But as she plucked each button and opened his shirt, his instincts overwhelmed him, forcing his hands around her slight wrists.

She has to stop.

It suddenly occurred to him just how different this would be, taking a woman face-to-face. The last time was over ten years ago. A quick bang from behind always avoided the inevitable questions, or comments, or expressions. No chance of puzzled glances. Or worse, pity.

But Madison was staying. He wanted her—all of her. Could he give all of himself in exchange?

Unable to move, he kept his hands around her wrists, helplessly locked in her gaze.

Smiling, she contemplated him with eyes filled with reassurance. He loosened his grip, and her still restrained hands moved through the unbuttoned portions of his shirt, slowly prying them apart.

She has to see it. See me.

Lightly, her fingers grazed the extensive scars that crossed from one side of his chest to the other. Her smile waned, but her eyes filled with tenderness as she freed another button.

"You want me to trust you?" she asked softly while sliding her hands through his grasp, beating him at his own game. Doing something unexpected.

Cautiously, she traced his wrists with her fingers, using the lesson he'd taught her to circle them and pivot the grasp to her control, sweetly forcing his surrender.

His muscles relaxed. His resistance disappeared. And slowly, he let her lower his arms, taking his hands in hers.

"Then trust me," she said, bringing the palm of his hand to her cheek before nuzzling it and pressing a kiss to his palm. Lovingly, she undid his cufflink. Again, she repeated her soft seduction.

Could he do anything but completely give in?

CHAPTER 28

MADISON

Instinctively, Madison understood. Whatever they were about to share would be new and unrivaled. And more beautiful than anything she'd experienced in her life.

In no hurry, she cherished their closeness, taking in his raw emotions and returning a feeling that filled her, spilling out into tender kisses and devouring him with every touch.

With the last button undone, she ran her hands over the firm angles of his abs, delicately moving them across the tight muscles of his chest. Unconcerned, she glided her fingers across his scars, and he let her. Shoving the shirt past his chiseled shoulders, she pushed it away, brushing a soft kiss to his lips as it fell to the floor.

Hooking her finger between his slacks and the heat of his skin, she tugged him closer, undoing his pants and releasing him from the rest of his clothes.

Naked, he stood before her, his chest heaving as he otherwise remained absolutely still. Madison ran her gaze from the angst of his eyes all the way down, taking him in with wonder and awe.

His body was magnificent. Perfect.

She licked her lips, again meeting his eyes in the hopes she could allay whatever negativity might be torturing him inside his head. Fear. Doubt. Hurt. The sliver of self-loathing breaking through. None of it mattered.

Eagerly, she explored him. Her hands drifted here and there over the faded tracks that marked him, before she laid light kisses along his chest, brushing her lips across all of him.

Swiftly, his hand wove through her hair, stopping her. The torment in his eyes melted. His mouth crashed against hers, invading her, his kiss rough and deep, taking her to the very brink with nothing more than his forceful tongue sweeping long strokes through her mouth.

As he tore her dress from her body, she heard the rips as his rushed hands moved carelessly, urgent with need. Still tightening his fist on her hair, he smoothed a strong hand over her sex, cupping it over the soaked wetness of her panties.

Standing before him in only her panties and heels, Madison lost herself in the heat of his touch. She was pulsing with need, ready to come right in his hand if this gorgeous god of a man wasn't careful.

With the lightest lick, he swirled her breast, then sucked in her nipple. As he forced a finger deep inside her, she moaned.

"Oh God."

The tender grip of his teeth on her nipple was too much. Her hips bucked, and she rode the burn of his hand uncontrollably.

Hurriedly, he grabbed a condom from the drawer and tore it free. Even with his finger sweetly fucking her, she needed to taste him first. She kicked off her heels and knelt before him. Sucking him in, she milked him gently with her mouth as she savored the scent and taste that were uniquely his. Satisfied, she took the condom and sheathed him with both hands, rolling it down his thick shaft.

Laying her back, Alex parted her legs, prying them open as he watched her arch, bracing for the pleasure to come. He inched out his finger, sucked it clean, and groaned low. The tip of him, firm and stiff, teased her opening, but he didn't press in.

Instead, he tore free the lace between her legs, tossing it aside as he pinned her down with his weight. The tip of him teased her, gliding back and forth before prying her swollen lips apart.

His thumb circled her sensitive clit, the pressure sending her higher. Panting, she fisted his hair. When he filled his mouth with the fullness of her breast, the sensation nearly sent her over the edge as his finger pushed past her tightness, again plunging deep inside.

"Alex!" She cried out, pleading with her tone as her body writhed beneath him. Desperate, she arched her back and wrapped her legs around him, ready to take absolutely everything this man had to give.

He teased her by withdrawing his finger, tracing her slick folds up and down with his shaft, forcing her to buck, begging shamelessly as she chased his cock with need and determination.

Finally, he pushed inside. As he shoved in every bit of his length, the air was forced from her lungs in a staggered cry. His width stretched her as he fucked her over and over, sweetly driving himself deeper.

Her wet folds engulfed him, the euphoria closing in on her as he shoved in to the hilt. With his thumb rubbing circles into her clit, her body rocked with him, clinging to every sensation as his lips seared her neck and shoulders. She sucked her own wetness from his lips as his mouth met hers. Then he pulled out.

"Please, Alex . . ."

The second she opened her eyes enough to meet his dark gaze, he sank deep inside her, splitting her wide in one swift move.

"Yes!" she cried as his cock tore through her.

Driving in and out, he hit her spot over and over until her nipples tightened painfully and her body shuddered. He wrecked her with each cruel pass, speeding up in a way that brought her to the brink before he slowed, settling her in a quiet ache only long enough to catch her breath.

Again, he pulled out, leaving just enough to cover his crown in her folds and slickness. Ready to finish the job herself, Madison had barely grazed the swollen lips of her pussy with her fingers when he yanked her arm high over her head, stretching her quivering body drenched in a sheen of sweat.

Her eyes met his dark, hungry gaze before his body crashed around her, tearing her into a thousand blissful pieces as he raced to a relentless rhythm.

"Now," he commanded, his voice low and stern as he rode her senseless and back again. "Come for me, Madison."

Her body erupted, obeying his gruff demand.

Alex jolted, his own climax catapulting her to the stratosphere as a second wave rushed through her, instantly tingling every nerve and filling her vision with clusters of stars. Her body shuddered as her walls tightened around him.

His mouth engulfed hers, muffling her raspy cries as he suckled her tongue and shattered her to oblivion.

Deep inside, she could feel him, pulsing desperately to empty all of himself inside her. Her muscles spasmed around him, milking him of everything he could give. With a final thrust, he pushed her beyond any fears or doubts, making her body light and her mind free until nothing else mattered.

I am his.

SIDE BY SIDE, Madison and Alex lay panting in the dark, holding hands. She was spent in every way. Physically. Emotionally. Her body was heavy and exhausted.

Alex took a deep breath and pulled her hand to his lips, brushing his mouth against her fingers before laying a kiss on her lips. "You sure you're not hungry? I could bring the food in here."

She shook her head, weaving her fingers tighter through his. "Alex, whatever it is you have to tell me, you can. I won't judge you."

Releasing a deep breath, he rolled to his back. She watched as he gazed at the ceiling, lost for a moment in thought. She followed, rolling herself on him, tangling her leg between his and laying soft kisses along his chest before nuzzling her head into his neck.

Softly, he stroked her hair, running his hands through it and down to the small of her back. Contented, he rested it there. With a kiss to her head, he began to speak.

"I'm guessing Paco spent the afternoon giving you a few lessons. Well, here's a lesson he taught me a long time ago." Pulling her hand to his lips, he kissed it, then clasped it to his chest. "Never make a promise you're not sure you can keep."

Madison's brow tightened as she took this in.

He's worried I'll judge him. Did he do something wrong? How wrong? Was it illegal? Immoral?

And what if he's right? What if I can't keep from judging him?

But she remained silent in the dark, thinking through what he'd said, certain that if Alex listened hard enough, he'd hear every wheel turn in her mind. And a lot of wheels were turning, spinning out of control with question after question.

A second later, Alex surprised her with a subdued chuckle that grew to a loud laugh.

Dumbfounded, she shot him a confused glare. "What?"

"So, do you remember our first encounter?"

Perplexed, Madison gave him a blank stare, her curiosity piqued. "No."

"Well, it's part of the reason we're together, but not all of it."

His quiet smirk was adorable. Intriguing.

Patiently, she waited for him to continue. Instead, he pulled his hands back neatly behind his head, seemingly satisfied to plant a seed with just enough water to grow.

"And?" Madison said hopefully.

"*And*, I have thirty days. You agreed. We sealed it with a kiss. And then some." He planted a small peck on her growing pout. Whispering to her lips, he said, "That's it for now."

"That's it?" Equally amused and annoyed, Madison asked, "Has anyone ever told you you're a tease?"

Grinning, he peered at her from the corner of his eye. "I've always wondered how to keep a drop-dead gorgeous woman in suspense. Now I know."

Flipping her willing body onto her back, he managed to draw a giggle from her as he gently rested his body on hers. For the moment, he quelled her light irritation with a kiss, melting every one of her emotions into pure submission.

This man will be the death of me.

Staring seriously into her eyes, he said, "Thirty days gives us time to get to know each other. But during that time, I want you to feel at home. Really at home. Have anything you desire at your beautiful little fingertips." He took each of her fingers to his lips, kissing them one by one.

Crinkling her nose, she shot him a look of pure determination. "Well, it might seem like a long time to be in suspense, but I'm not going to be distracted by all this glitz and glamour," she said, exuding a hard-core, take-no-prisoners demeanor. Insistent, she handed him the terms. "You have exactly thirty days, Mr. Drake."

Warmly, he kissed her again. "Thirty days." He saluted smartly, then continued. "I won't let you down, Ms. Taylor."

You'd better not, Alex Drake.

And with that, they began another round of consummating their month-long deal.

~

THANK YOU FOR READING *ACCESS*! I hope you love Alex and Madison as much as I do. (And, of course, Paco!) *Ready to know the deep, dark secrets Alex has been hiding from Madison?* **Get EXPOSED Now!**

Keep going to read the first few chapters.

Join Lexxi's VIP reader list to be the first to know of new releases, free books, special prices, and other giveaways!

Free hot romances & happily ever afters delivered to your inbox.
https://www.lexxijames.com/freebies

IF YOU LOVED ACCESS, you'll love Fallen Dom.

For Jake Russo, abandoning the past became his only future. It should have been his burden alone. But he had one cross to bear. Watching over Kathryn Chase . . . in secret.

Her unangelic guardian paying back a debt.

Available on All Platforms! **Get FALLEN DOM now!**

LOOKING FOR ANOTHER SEXY BILLIONAIRE? Meet Davis R. Black . . . aka Richard. Some know him as a tech mogul. To Jaclyn, he's the King of the A-holes. Which is why this billionaire is hiding *his* in plain sight. Check out the first book in the Ruthless Billionaires Club.

Available on All Platforms! **Get RUTHLESS GAMES now!**

EXPOSED

AN ALEX DRAKE NOVEL

CHAPTER 1

MADISON

"So, who is he?"

Madison caught the sly tone in her best friend's knowing voice. Sheila might be a reporter for the *New York Times*, but today her investigative skills were focused on getting the goods on Madison—her best friend and soon-to-be maid of honor.

Patiently, Sheila skated her finger along the rim of her half-consumed latte, her eyes dancing with anticipation as she waited.

Making a casual turn away, Madison focused on scanning the city streets from their perch at the corner café. Avoiding Sheila's see-right-through-you eye contact at all costs was pretty much impossible with the superhuman weight of her stare.

Madison shrugged, her lips breaking the leaf-decorated foam of her cappuccino as she savored an extra-long sip from the oversize mug. "I'm not sure what you mean."

"Right," Sheila drawled. As if ready to expose a cover-up, the diligent reporter leaned in. "Sure. The ridiculous smiling. The pep in your step. The glowing skin. I get it. You want to keep it on the down low. But you know that sooner or later, I'll figure out who he is."

Undoubtedly, Sheila was right. Always accurate in reading Madison's deepest thoughts, it didn't help that Sheila was a legitimate bloodhound when it came to sniffing out the truth. And keeping secrets was the last thing Madison wanted.

But sharing her secret with anyone, let alone an up-and-coming reporter like Sheila, was completely out of the question.

With a meditative breath, Madison let Sheila attempt her Jedi mind tricks, maintaining a stoic poker face. Madison rarely kept things from her best friend, and she knew Sheila was probably putting two and two together as they sat. With where Madison worked and how long she'd been floating on air, perhaps she was naive to think her new relationship with her boss would stay under wraps. But if Sheila figured it out on her own, it was fair game.

"Wait!" Sheila bounced in her chair, the riddle solved. "Holy shit, I get it. I know your big secret. You're dating . . ."

Madison sucked in a deep breath, ready for Alex Drake's name to fall from Sheila's lips. If Sheila connected the dots, Madison couldn't possibly deny it. Not convincingly, anyway. Instead, she braced for impact, her head already in an anticipatory nod of agreement before Sheila finished her sentence.

"A woman."

"Yes . . . *what?*" Madison's shy smile and modest blush vanished as she mentally repeated the last few lines of their conversation. *Did I just acknowledge being in a relationship with a woman?*

As Madison's head quickly shifted from nodding to shaking, Sheila's tone was reassuring.

"Look, if you're not ready to come out, I'm a vault. But really, we'd all be good with it." As Madison clasped her hands and placed her elbows on the table, leaning forward to correct the misunderstanding, Sheila piled her hands on top. "We're happiest when you're happy, and you're obviously happy."

Madison weighed the cards she held. On one hand, if she protested, Sheila and their other friends would just keep pestering her for her new significant other's identity. And it wasn't as if Alex had urged her to keep it under wraps. He hadn't.

If anything, he'd always made suggestions for them to go out. In public. Where absolutely anyone and everyone could see them. Together.

Just the thought made Madison's arms itch, but she resisted the urge to scratch. The truth was, she just wasn't ready to share this secret. Instead, she held it close, preserving the precious revelation like cherishing a wish in the seconds before blowing out the candles of a birthday cake.

On the other hand, perhaps playing along was the path of least resistance. Satiated for the moment, her friends would at least give her some breathing space. The ploy would buy a little time to get to know Alex better. In private.

And it wouldn't be an outright lie, would it? Madison didn't exactly say she was dating a woman. Sheila did. Madison could just, well, conveniently not deny it.

Tugging her hands delicately away like a Jenga piece, she gave her friend a smile.

"Well, um . . . I'm not saying I'm with a woman," she said, and Sheila blinked at her in confusion. "And I'm not saying I'm with a man . . . um . . . in particular." Madison's answer was becoming so tangled, she started confusing herself.

"So, you're not with anyone?" With a suspicious squint and lifted brow, Sheila took a slow sip of her drink.

Madison swallowed the lump in her throat, desperate to mask her every tell. Was it working?

As if sensing her uncertainty, Sheila stared back, studying Madison and searching her eyes for a clue to the truth.

I hate lying. Not just because it's deceptive and wrong, but because I suck at it.

Could she backpedal without tripping up? "Perhaps it's best I leave it at that."

"Leave it at what?" Sheila strummed her fingers on the table until she froze and her eyes lit up with enthusiasm. "Oh, you're *curious.*"

Sheila's slow, assured nod nearly convinced Madison to go ahead and confess. But she resisted. Wanting to avoid another ride on this merry-go-round of a guessing game, Madison decided to settle into her new label. At least for the time being.

I mean, it's true. By nature, I am a curious person. Sheila obviously inferred Madison's bi-curious status. *But that's not what I said.*

Newly attuned to the fine print, Madison spoke carefully. "I'm curious in general, sure." Her reply sounded much more like a question than a statement, but she went with it.

Squealing with delight, Sheila caught herself. Knocking her enthusiasm down half a peg, she leaned in closer. "Hey, I get it. I've dabbled in, you know, curiosity."

Choking on her froth, Madison widened her eyes, panicked that Sheila was undoubtedly ready to unburden herself with a rich assortment of endless and highly detailed visual descriptions.

Luckily, the waiter broke in. *Thank God.*

"Ladies, can I get you anything else?" Swooping between the two of them, he cleared the emptied plates.

Relieved, Madison breathed her sigh through a smile, never imagining how thankful she'd be for an interruption to girl talk. "Sheila, I've really got to get back to work." Reaching for her latest Hermès clutch, she pulled out the matching wallet, prepared to pay the bill.

"No, no, no, girl. This one's on me," Sheila said, handing the waiter cash. "No change, thanks."

"Thank *you*, ma'am," he said, delighted with the fat tip as he carried the neat stack of plates and cups away.

Both ladies stood. Madison stepped over, not fully prepared for Sheila's sweeping hug, which lingered as she happily rocked Madison to and fro before leaning back.

"And if you ever need to talk with someone who's, you know, been *there*," Sheila glanced at their crotches, "I'm here for you."

Madison followed Sheila's eye movements before snapping hers shut, desperate to kill whatever image might intrude into her thoughts. *That which has been thought can't be un-thought.*

"Okay, then," Madison said hesitantly. "I do so appreciate that, girl. Well, gotta run."

Madison checked her ten-carat diamond bracelet as if it were a watch, intent on scampering away. Extricating herself from the warm hug, she turned to head off, propelled faster with the light smack of Sheila's hand on her ass.

"You do you, girl!" Sheila called out a little too loudly for Madison's comfort. "And bring whoever you want to the wedding."

Madison waved back awkwardly, lowering her head while letting her thick tresses drape over her burning cheeks as she headed down the street.

As she approached the towering skyscraper that housed Drake Global Industries' New York City headquarters, she marveled at how her life had become an unbelievable whirlwind over the past few weeks. The dinners. The shopping. The traveling. It was overwhelming, but she'd done her best to take every bit of the opulence in stride.

Alex Drake had money. That much was clear. But as strange as it sounded, the lavish lifestyle this billionaire could afford her wasn't nearly as appealing as the man himself.

It was hard not to be a fangirl in his presence, but Madison cherished every here-and-there opportunity to get to know the reclusive man better. Those moments weren't showy or lavish, and they meant everything. How he managed to make mundane, everyday life feel new and magical was beyond her.

He adored her as no one had, as if she were the first woman to really be in his life. *And maybe I am*. But was there a reason for that? She tamped down her anxiety as much as she could, but it stubbornly remained in the back of her mind, threatening to come front and center at the slightest bump in the road of their relationship.

And as much as their blossoming relationship was wonderful, it was all so private. Extremely private. It wasn't as if they'd signed a nondisclosure agreement or anything, but neither of them pressed the other too hard to shout their relationship from the rooftops.

Madison wasn't eager to go public. She knew her credibility might fly out the window at DGI if water-cooler gossip hit the halls about her personal relationship with the boss. And Alex just seemed contented to keep her all to himself. Who could blame him?

And if things between them detoured from happily-ever-after, not only his image, but DGI's as well, might suffer an unintended consequence or two. Or a million. On top of which, their relationship was all so new. Only a few weeks.

Now, by the calendar of public opinion, some might argue this alone was more than impressive. It represented an Alex Drake Olympic-level world record. A notorious bachelor and womanizer, a Drake month of dating might as well be a dog year.

But worst of all, there was the secrecy. Maybe *secrecy* was too strong a term, but why was he waiting to tell her "everything else," as he put it?

What else is there? And what's with the book? And the photo? Or how we met? Or the whole making myself "at home" in his lap of luxury?

She'd noticed the novel *The Count of Monte Cristo* in his penthouse home, an inscribed gift many years ago from her grandpa Mike. Why would Alex have it? And the mysterious photo of her as a bright-eyed teen in one of the last moments with her dad before her parents' divorce. Why couldn't she remember it?

Shocking revelations had been piling up, kept just out of reach. When Madison demanded answers, Alex gave none. None in that moment, and none for the next month. But in thirty days, she'd have all her answers. All she had to do was stick around. And in a show of good faith, he handed her a contract. One she couldn't refuse.

I, Alex Drake, being of sound mind, do hereby agree that if I ever lie to Madison Taylor, everything I have and everything I own, including my personal and corporate holdings, will immediately and unequivocally be transferred to her for whatever purpose she deems fit.

Obviously, the man was insane. And just like that, Madison had moved in with him. How could she not? Because they were a perfect match—her crazy to his insanity. Could he possibly know he was the first man she'd ever lived with?

Normally, she'd have towering emotional walls built high around herself, preventing anyone from getting too close. Always protecting herself from a life where loss was inevitable. But with Alex, there were no walls. She'd eased into his life with cozy familiarity and had never been so comfortable. So at home. It should really bother her, but it didn't. At least, not enough for her to leave.

I'm falling. Hard. For a man I barely know. Which makes me certifiable. Possibly idiotic. But the thirty days I promised him are nearly up, so ready or not, answers are coming.

Despite all the other questions that pelted her mind daily, none of these was the most significant. The biggest remained the undisputed heavyweight question of all time.

Why me?

As quickly as these questions arose day in and day out, Madison just as persistently whack-a-moled them down. Per their agreement, all her answers were only a few days away. With that, she opted to focus instead on the monster of a question at hand.

Sheila's wedding was right around the corner. Madison was the maid of honor, and a plus-one would be required. The question of the hour danced through her mind.

Should I bring a man, or a woman?

CHAPTER 2

MADISON

Fidgeting, Madison stood as solemnly as possible in front of her boss's desk, desperate to keep a straight face.

"Let me get this straight." Alex sat at his desk, resting his elbows comfortably on the arms of his custom-made leather chair as his fingers steepled to his chin. A cocky-ass smirk spread across his face, drawing out a smile of her own that Madison couldn't hide. "You want to date a woman?"

"No!" she exclaimed, rolling her eyes at his misunderstanding.

"Oh, you just want to dip your *toe* in to test the waters. Or is this more of a *plunge* into the deep end?" Exaggerating a swan dive with one hand, he slid the fingers into the grip of the other, then suggestively pushed his fingers in and out of the clasped hole.

Madison shook her head, ignoring the heat his provocative miming stirred beneath her skirt. Sure, she was annoyed—more at herself than at Alex. Mostly because she couldn't hold back a laugh, no matter how she tried.

When Alex stood up, straightening and buttoning his blazer in that completely normal and sexier-than-hell way he always did, she bit her lip. He strolled around his desk to her, and her breath hitched as his warm and somewhat patriarchal hand landed her shoulder.

His expression somber, he cleared his throat. "Seriously, I support you. And if you need an innocent bystander to walk you through the delicate intricacies of pleasuring a woman, well . . . count me in." His selfless offer and cheesy grin were incorrigible.

God, he's such a man.

But he wasn't done. Lifting her hands, he held them against his chest. "Whatever you need, just name it." His deep tone coupled with those mesmerizing eyes somehow always made him less annoying and more adorable.

And don't even get me started on that boyish naughty grin.

Pulling her close, he lightly rubbed her nose with his. A delicate peck on her lips came next, which led to the most irresistible kisses down her neck.

"Well, there is *something* I need," Madison said, trying not to submit completely to Alex's intoxicating advances. *Though my panties are melted to oblivion.*

"Mm-hmm. Name it, you kinky little vixen." Alex made his way lower, rumbling out a delighted moan as he left a trail of searing kisses between her breasts. Cupping her fullness from the outside, he pressed her cleavage to his softly whiskered face.

Madison's breathing stuttered, partially from the touch of his lips rubbing across her décolletage, but mostly from the butterflies filling her stomach. "I need . . ."

"Yes? What do you need?" His tone was low and deep as he stood tall again, his hands making their way to the round curve of her ass, pulling her into him. His firm erection pressed against her skirt, coaxing her core and making her wetter by the second.

"I need a date for the wedding, but . . ." Exasperated, Madison let out a breath, averting her eyes. Her gaze dropped to his desk, seeing the penny she'd left weeks ago still in place. The heads-up coin stared back at her, reminding her to stay true to her feelings while guilting the hell out of her. She struggled to finish her sentence.

Alex pulled back, ducking his head down just enough to catch her gaze. Again, she tried looking away. His fingers lifted her chin, encouraging her eyes to meet his.

"But?"

A slow sigh escaped her lips, releasing a buildup of low, continuous pressure she'd been holding in.

"But I'm not sure we're ready for a public appearance." Searching his eyes, she forced out the last of her words. "Are you?"

With a fresh set of those damn nervous hives prickling up her arm, Madison waited, apprehension filling her as she waited for his reply.

READY TO KNOW THE DEEP, *dark secrets Alex has been hiding from Madison?* **Get EXPOSED Now!**

ABOUT THE AUTHOR

Lexxi James is a best-selling author of romantic suspense. Her feats in multi-tasking include binge watching Netflix and sucking down a cappuccino in between feverish typing and loads of laundry.

She lives in Ohio with her teen daughter and the sweetest man in the universe. She loves to hear from readers!

www.LexxiJames.com